SARATOGA
FLESHPOT

Books By Stephen Dobyns

Poetry

Velocities: New and Selected Poems, 1966–92 (1994)
Body Traffic (1990)
Cemetery Nights (1987)
Black Dog, Red Dog (1984)
The Balthus Poems (1982)
Heat Death (1980)
Griffon (1976)
Concurring Beasts (1972)

Novels

Saratoga Fleshpot (1995)
Saratoga Backtalk (1994)
The Wrestler's Cruel Study (1993)
Saratoga Haunting (1993)
After Shocks/Near Escapes (1991)
Saratoga Hexameter (1990)
The House on Alexandrine (1990)
Saratoga Bestiary (1988)
The Two Deaths of Señora Puccini (1988)
A Boat off the Coast (1987)
Saratoga Snapper (1986)
Cold Dog Soup (1985)
Saratoga Headhunter (1985)
Dancer with One Leg (1983)
Saratoga Swimmer (1981)
Saratoga Longshot (1976)
A Man of Little Evils (1973)

SARATOGA FLESHPOT

Stephen
Dobyns

W.W. Norton & Company
New York London

The text of this book is composed in Bembo 227
with the display set in Modula
Composition and manufacturing by the Haddon Craftsmen, Inc.
Book design by Chris Welch

Library of Congress Cataloging-in-Publication Data
Dobyns, Stephen, 1941–
Saratoga Fleshpot / Stephen Dobyns.
p.   cm.
I. Title.
PS3554.02S253   1995
813'.54—dc20   95-1726

ISBN 0-393-03805-X

W. W. Norton & Company, Inc., 500 Fifth Avenue, New York, N.Y. 10010
W. W. Norton & Company Ltd., 10 Coptic Street, London WC1A 1PU

1   2   3   4   5   6   7   8   9   0

For Stuart Dischell

The two meet
After work for games of chance then to drink
And eat at their favorite bar. Alternately one buys
The other's meal and the other leaves the tip.
It's a system they've invented over years of friendship,
Like one hand washing the other, you scratching
My back and me scratching yours, and other sayings
They are fond of saying. Most nights they talk
About their childhoods and current difficulties.
They describe in detail what they think and feel
Concerning the waitress's rear end. They're buddies,
Pals, boon companions.

—from "Buddies"
Stuart Dischell

SARATOGA
FLESHPOT

1

I named the horse Fleshpot because he kept trying to grab my ass, take a little nip with his big white teeth. It was pure friendliness on his part. A chestnut colt with a white left front stocking and a white blaze on his forehead shaped like the state of New Jersey. He liked me so much that he wanted to see how I'd taste. He wanted to roll me around on his tongue. I've had girlfriends who hankered to do the same thing. And it was because Fleshpot had this passionate attraction to my backside that events turned out as they did and various crimes were uncovered. In such a way can the peculiar cravings of a four-footed creature betray the misdeeds of the two-footed ones. But I am getting ahead of myself.

My name is Victor Plotz and I am an entrepreneur in Saratoga Springs, New York. That is, I used to be an entrepreneur: fast-moving stocks, cattle market futures, hog bellies, buy low in the morning, sell high at night. I had some ladies who trusted me with their cash and over the years I had built up a golden nest egg of my own. I was Mr. High Finance, Mr. Big Bucks. But all that was before the stock market crash.

Let me say that the crash of '94 had a very narrow focus. I got hit, maybe a couple of others. It was like chalk marks on a blackboard—I got erased. Worse, my ladies took to doubting my expertise and demanded their money back. Hey, I told them, you lost money, I lost money too. My nest egg was depleted. My credibility exhausted. My reputation shot. But it could have been worse. My friend Charlie Bradshaw says I was lucky to stay out of jail. It seems that I had made promises I couldn't keep. I can't remember. My mind goes blank. In any case, I got visited by lawyers and plainclothes coppers who kept bandying about the word "fraud" so that it hung in the air like an inflatable shuttlecock. Were there skyscrapers in Saratoga Springs, I might of hopped out of a high window. But Saratoga is a town of squat, stubby buildings and I figured if I jumped I'd only bust my ankle, so I got drunk instead.

All this was back in June. I lost my Mercedes. My four duplexes returned to the bank. Some furniture got repossessed. I'd bought a nice cottage out on Lake Saratoga so I could be near my pal Charlie Bradshaw and the bank snatched that as well. I was lucky that the lawyers didn't take my cat. The coppers even had a warrant to search my apartment. Do you know what it's like to have strange hands rummaging through your sock drawer? To tell the truth, I had a few bucks hidden away in a safe spot but if I publicized this fact, I'd lose that money as well. My own lawyer curled his lip at me and called me a doofus. It's not that I could just start over again. I'm about sixty or thereabouts and I've already been about sixty for a few years. Consequently, toward the end of July I was knocking on Charlie Bradshaw's office door looking for a job, nothing permanent you understand, just something to tide me over and make me look good with the authorities. I mean, if I didn't work to look humble and beaten, somebody might have guessed that I had money tucked away, and I couldn't afford that. I'm not the kind of guy who poverty looks good on.

Charlie Bradshaw is a private detective and before that he was a cop. I guess he was a cop for twenty years and now he has been a detective for almost as long. He's not a big guy and he's not a ferocious guy and he doesn't know squat about fancy wines or cigars and the car he drives is a Mazda 323, a pipsqueak of a car. Nowadays he makes most of his money from insurance cases, checking into fires and claims that might be fraudulent. Then he does some low-level missing persons work—husbands on a fling, daughters run off with a boyfriend—and over the years he has made some contacts with the horse crowd and sometimes he provides security for some horse owner or anything that requires a sharp pair of eyes. Unlike me, Charlie is not a guy with a lot of ambition. He moves along at a certain pace and I tend to lap him, sort of like the tortoise and the hare. And that comparison is right on the money, because it wasn't Charlie who was hurting after the crash of '94. Haste, Charlie likes to say to me, makes waste. Then he smiles.

Charlie has got a seedy-looking office on Phila Street over a used-book store and across the street from a dentist. The single thing in its favor is that the Ben & Jerry's ice cream shop is only half a block away. The office has a little anteroom with some *National Geographics* from the used-book store downstairs and a bunch of dead flies who probably scragged themselves out of boredom. The day in question was a Friday, shortly after lunch. The summer stint of thoroughbred racing was to start next week and already the town was getting crowded: eager losers hoping to be winners. It used to be I'd rent out my duplexes during the five weeks of racing season and make a bundle, but now I didn't have that property anymore. If you think that sixty or there-abouts is an unfortunate age to be dead broke, you hit the nail on the head. It was hard for me to stay chipper, to keep a smile on my lips and a song in my heart. I needed gainful employment and I didn't care what kind.

I rapped on the glass that says "office" and entered without waiting for a reply. Doors, right? Aren't they a mystery? Here I expected to find Charlie sitting at his desk reading up on some old outlaw who had caught his fancy—Deadeye Dick or Rapscallion Ralph—and instead he was smooching with his girlfriend, Janey Burris. Considering how he reacted, you'd think I'd caught him with his pants down.

"Jesus, Victor, can't you knock?"

"I did but you were too caught up in your passion."

Janey grinned at me. I figured she had just been attending one of those noon aerobics classes at the YMCA because she was wearing a blue tank top and shorts and her ragged black hair looked damp. She's a good-looking nurse in her forties with the body of a gymnast, which to me means too much bone and gristle. Sleeping with her would be like sleeping on a futon. I like a woman with no hard edges, a woman who spills over at the sides, a featherbed kind of woman. But I'm fond of Janey and if she gained forty pounds I might glance at her more than once.

Charlie still looked exasperated, which makes his gray hair stick up in peaks. He was wearing a white short-sleeved shirt that was a trifle threadbare, shiny blue slacks that probably started life as a gusher of oil and a striped necktie that must have been the veteran of a dozen suicide attempts. You know those Before and After pictures in certain advertisements? Charlie could make a bundle by portraying the Before part of the ad. Around his mouth, just like a Barnum and Bailey clown, was a red smear from Janey's lip gloss.

"Charlie, I need a job," I said. "If I don't get something right away the savage lawyers will think I've got money hidden someplace."

Charlie sat back in his chair and Janey scrambled off his desk and straightened her shorts. The nice thing about friends is they forgive you, although you don't want to push it too hard. Charlie looked at me thoughtfully and made a little tent out of the fingers of both hands. He's got big blue eyes half concealed by a pair of bifocals and a round face as smooth as a baby's rump. Right now he's someplace in his mid-fifties. He had a birthday back in April and I threw a party with two hundred guests, half of whom had jail time on their vitae. That was when I was still flush. You've heard of the Mississippi Scheme and the South Sea Bubble? I was the Vic Plotz Bubble.

"What kind of job do you need?" asked Janey.

"Something to make me look honest and humble."

"Have you thought of entering a monastery?" asked Charlie.

He likes his little joke. You know how kids will drive you crazy with knock-knock jokes and asking where the sheep gets his hair cut? It's like that. But if you don't encourage the little tykes, they never develop a sense of humor and they grow up to become serial killers, or worse.

"They wouldn't allow conjugal visits from the Queen of Softness," I told him. That's my girlfriend, but more about her later. "Seriously, Charlie, I got to make it seem that I'm hauling myself up by my bootstraps."

So he thought about it and Janey Burris thought about it too. Charlie's office is a barren sort of place with an old desk and visitor's chair, green linoleum on the floor, a file cabinet and an antique safe where he keeps his revolver. For some time I've been urging him to get a computer but the idea seems to frighten him. I tell him that he wouldn't need to use it but the computer would give his customers confidence. On the wall behind his desk between the two windows looking out on Phila Street, Charlie has hung a poster-size photo of Jesse James in an ornate Victorian frame. Jesse has a birdlike face, not one of those birds that tweedles, rather the kind that snatches mice and voles away from their law-abiding errands. For Charlie, Jesse James is a guy who did what he wanted to do when he wanted to do it. No lesson plans for him. No social security payments. No insurance forms. Jesse was a guy against whom nagging never worked, until he got shot, of course.

"What about a job at my mother's hotel?" asked Charlie.

"Washing dishes?"

"Busing tables."

"That's a trifle too humble, Charlie. Besides, your mother can't stand me." Charlie's mother runs the Bentley, right on Broadway in downtown Saratoga: one of those hotels where you walk through the front doors and suddenly it's the 1880s but with antibiotics and TVs hidden in the armoires. I worked there for a while as assistant manager, winter caretaker and hotel detective: three different stints, three different painful memories. Charlie's mother claims I nearly put the hotel into receivership. I tell her that it's a source of pride on my part that I don't suffer fools gladly.

"I could probably get you a job at the hospital," said Janey. She stood with her hand on Charlie's shoulder. She had a husband once but he ran off to Australia. Sometimes he sends her postcards with pictures of sheep ranches with the message: "Wish you were here."

"Would I have to see blood?"

"Not necessarily."

"Even swellings upset me."

So that was how it went for a while. Charlie or Janey would suggest some humiliating form of employment and I would find a flaw. Yard work would wreak havoc with my hay fever. ("I didn't know you had hay fever," said Charlie. "I just got it," I told him.) Working in a men's clothing store would be bad on my arches and besides I had done that for twenty years in New York City and if I ever did it again I'd go berserk. Working in the kitchen of a chowhouse would give me pimples.

"What about a lifeguard at a pool?" I asked.

"Do you swim?"

"I could learn."

Then Charlie thought of a couple of surveillance jobs where I got to watch a doorway for forty-eight hours a day. No thanks.

"Baby-sitting?" suggested Janey.

"I'm not good with kids," I said. "I get them riled up."

"I've an idea," said Charlie. He picked up the phone and dialed a number. Janey and I stared at him. To tell you the truth, I was beginning to lose confidence. Somebody picked up on the other end and Charlie went through half a minute of boy talk about the Red Sox and life in the trenches. Then he asked, "Are you still looking for someone for that security job?" He paused, nodded, then said, "I think I've got the right guy for you."

"What kind of security job?" I asked when he had hung up the phone. I'm a little overweight, a little out of shape, and the only rassling I do these days is with the Queen of Softness.

"It's over at the yearling sales," he said. "You know, the horse auctions?"

"Do I guard the horses? I thought the Pinkertons did that."

"No, not the horses."

"Do I guard the people, all the fat cats and pretty women?"

"No, not the people."

"Do I keep an eye on the tables and chairs? Keep the lowlifes from swiping the bar glasses?"

"No, nothing like that."

"Then what the hell do I do, Charlie?"

"You know the Humphrey S. Finney Pavilion where they auction the horses? Well, they're putting up an exhibit of nineteenth-century English and French paintings on the second floor. Paintings of horses and racetracks, landscapes and portraits. Henry Brown Limited from London. They're hoping to sell quite a few. They need someone to guard the paintings."

So that was how it started.

2

I don't know if you have ever guarded paintings before, but it can be tiresome work. I mean, after you've looked at them ten times, they become so much wallpaper. They don't talk, they don't make jokes or give you a sly wink. And these paintings depicted a life that won't be seen again on this earth: lazy summer afternoons on English farms with a kid in fancy duds walking a leggy horse from a thatched barn, Derby Day scenes with the women with parasols and wearing antique clothes that covered every inch of their skin but the pale circles of their faces. Maybe there were one hundred and twenty of them. It was pretty stuff but even the cheapest started at five grand. A young blond woman named Fletcher with an accent like breakable crystal told me what to do (to walk back and forth authoritatively but to speak to no one and get in nobody's way), then drifted off to check her makeup. Until the yearling sales started in two weeks' time, it seemed I would hardly have any company, except workmen and the odd browser. I didn't even get to carry a pistol.

I showed up at noon on Monday and practiced my casual

walk for eight hours. Ms. Fletcher had provided me with a brown uniform that gave me a vaguely military air. It was brown, I figured, because the company name was Brown: Henry Brown Limited of London. I felt lucky his name wasn't Henry Magenta or Henry Chartreuse. I also had a brown baseball cap. I got fuzzy hair, like somewhere back on my family tree is a dandelion clock. This brown baseball cap had "Henry Brown Limited" printed in yellow across the front and it didn't so much fit upon my head as rest on my hair like a surfboard rests upon the sea. It also kept falling off. Sometimes I pinned the cap to my hair like a yarmulke but mostly I just carried it in my hand except when Ms. Fletcher was nearby.

The Pavilion is a round building of naked concrete. Inside are two levels of red plush seats. The very rich people sit in the twelve rows downstairs, the moderately rich sit in the four rows upstairs. No prospective buyer gets in without a credit check. The rows make half a circle with the auction ring and the auctioneer's pulpit in the very center. The pictures I was guarding hung on the wall behind the last seats on the second floor and above the auction ring. Also above the auction ring was a press box and a big electric sign suspended from the ceiling that said *Fasig-Tipton Saratoga* on top and *1994 Selected Yearlings* on the bottom. In between would flash the current bid on a particular yearling and then the closing price. All told that year there were one hundred and ninety yearlings with about sixty-five being auctioned each night: the seventy-fourth annual yearling sales in Saratoga Springs. Some of the horses might bring thirty grand, some upwards of a million, with the average coming in at a hundred thousand. Not bad for an adolescent that has never had a saddle on his back.

But in these first days before the sales, I was about the only activity in the Pavilion, or rather the paintings were, as well as some folks cleaning and putting pink geraniums in the flower boxes. At the back of the balcony, right across from the auction-eer's pulpit, was a bronze bust of Humphrey S. Finney himself, complete with buck teeth and reading glasses, the Brit after whom the Pavilion was named and who had conducted the auctions for so long. He was my main company, and when I wandered by I patted his head.

Ms. Fletcher was the saleslady, or agent as she liked to be called. She was one of those women who dislikes chitchat and when I asked about the possibility of me making a sale and getting a commission, she led me to understand that Elvis would rise from his grave and sing "I've Been Working on the Railroad" before that was likely to happen. She was as cold-hearted as a Gila monster and twice as shiny. I don't know what she did for boyfriends, probably chummied up to a parking meter. I guessed she was thirty-five going on ninety.

Unfortunately, I needed the job. Even my lawyer said he would send me packing unless I had gainful employment and starting attending synagogue. He whispered the words "grand jury" as others might whisper the words "acid bath." The authorities seemed to think that I had sold the exact same stock shares to several different old ladies. A silly idea. But it required me to put up with Ms. Fletcher's chilly exterior and save the backtalk for my dreams. I had to be deferential, generous, sweet-talking and humble. It's unfair. When Christians act like that they get made into saints.

But I was not completely alone, and here is where the complications began. In order to push the humility gimmick as far as Bad Breath, Idaho, I had got myself a little bicycle, one of those black three-speed British jobbies, that looked as if it had once swum the Channel: rusty. Maybe it was a dozen blocks from my apartment in the Algonquin on Broadway over to the Humphrey S. Finney Pavilion on East Avenue right across from the Oklahoma Track, now used as a training track. They say that once you learn to ride a bike you never forget. I didn't find that to be true. They could have called me Mr. Wobble. Because I proceeded forward in a violent zigzag and needed a lot of space, I took only the back streets. I would have gotten killed on Lake Avenue. Grove to York to Harrison to Caroline to Ludlow to Madison: the names of those streets are embossed upon the tissues of my heart. That was how I happened to see him.

I suppose one should feel flattered to be followed. It means there is something special about you. No longer are you part of the hoi polloi. Sad to say a person is rarely followed because of his good qualities, but for his transgressions. Even that can be flattering if one is followed by a real pro, a genius of surveillance. I mean, these guys must be paid according to their skills and Einstein racks up more bucks than Yogi Bear. But the guy following me would have made even Yogi Bear look good.

I expect I would have seen him even if I had gone straight down Lake Avenue, but maybe not as quickly. Because of my twists and turns, I spotted him on my very first day. But if you are going to follow somebody, does it make sense to drive an antique lime-green Volkswagen bug with a raccoon tail attached to the radio antenna? From this I deduced that this guy was also in the business of making me realize I was being followed, which made his following a form of bullying. Like I figured he had been employed by the lawyers of my enemies to throw a scare into me. It didn't do that but I began to think I had made an error in the self-image I had eagerly projected to my former clients.

When I was in the business of convincing old ladies to trust me with their cash, I had gone far to give the impression that I was as rich as Croesus. Since I had billions myself, why should I interest myself in their paltry thousands but out of the kindness of my heart, right? And this was an innocent deception at which I excelled. I sent my ladies red roses, I sent them Godiva chocolates. In fact, I excelled too well, because when the crash of '94 knocked me for a loop and I was rendered almost penniless, my protestations of poverty were not believed. True, I did have a few nickels and dimes tucked away, but nothing like the fortune that the lawyers of my enemies assumed I had. And this twerp in the lime-green Volkswagen with the raccoon tail attached to the antenna who poked along about ten feet behind my Raleigh— his job was apparently to so terrify me that I would have a moral epileptic fit and confess my sins.

This guy was about twenty-two and he had short pale blond hair brushed up in front to make a small replica of the chalk cliffs of Dover. He was chubby without being fat and his face resembled a pink dinner plate from Syracuse china. In order to look cool, he wore a blue denim shirt and a red necktie. I didn't even have to look at his feet to know he was wearing Timberland handsewn moccasins.

I should say that even though I didn't drive to the Pavilion, I did have a motorized vehicle: a two-tone 1987 Yugo, half red and half rust. If you are into humility, nothing beats a Yugo. When you are chugging down the street, you can see people turn toward you and silently mouth the word "sap." But I didn't quite fit into the Yugo—it bumped my bones in an unwholesome way—and to tell the truth, the Raleigh felt safer.

The art exhibit opened on Monday of the first week of racing. There had been a party Sunday night but I didn't get invited and Ms. Fletcher didn't confide in me when I asked if it had been a blowout. The retard in the lime-green Beetle followed me to the Pavilion, then hung around outside, buffing his nails and smoking Merit Lights. I love these guys with their gimmicks swiped from a movie or TV show. Like their gestures, their clothing, their facial expression show a sense of correctness that even a nun couldn't match. But it's like a two-dimensional movie set and you wonder who is hanging out in the back lot:

some pimply kid with his jeans hardly reaching his ankles and white socks. When I pedaled home that evening, Sherlock Holmes followed me, and when I pedaled back to the Pavilion shortly before noon on Tuesday, there he was again with his pink face and no-affect stare.

On Tuesday the track is dark. I guess it's that way all over the country. Maybe it's a religious holiday for the horses. They all say a prayer to Pegasus or whoever. Ms. Fletcher said we could expect a crowd at the Pavilion but if fifty people makes up a crowd, then I'm an artichoke. Still, I got to practice my guardian-of-art moves. Whenever anyone got within two feet of a picture, I'd come running up, clear my throat like Vesuvius on the prowl and rapidly raise and lower my eyebrows. That was interesting for a while. Then I took to making witty remarks like "Art lives forever only if you don't touch it" and "Are you looking at that painting or hoping to mate with it?"—that was when someone got really close. With all this folderol the time passed pleasantly and the next day I hoped to bring a whistle with which to make a piercing shriek. Around four, I got a half-hour break and Ms. Fletcher came to spell me. She was a student of the curt nod school and once I got the nod I knew I'd been freed for precisely thirty minutes.

When I got outside, I saw Sherlock Holmes leaning against a small tree behind the Pavilion and learning to blow smoke rings. The Pavilion is almost completely round, with the front half for the people and the back half for the horses and bathrooms. Behind the Pavilion is a big walking ring covered with green-and-white-striped canvas where the horses try to relax before they are taken inside. Then there is a long two-story green building with horses (empty stalls at this point) on the bottom and Fasig-Tipton offices on top. Across from it and the walking ring is a long low white ranch-house-type building with other offices, security, banks of telephones and the stuff that runs the day-today business. And behind all that are the fancy green shed rows or barns that probably accommodate about two hundred and fifty horses. Some of these farms or agents that show up to sell yearlings might bring twenty horses, others might bring only two or three. But in every case this is the money that keeps the farms in business and so they are eager.

Then there are little bunkhouses and a blacksmith shop and a kitchen, then a fancy bar and restaurant for the rich folks and a snack bar for the lesser lights. And trees, lots of trees. I could see that it would be a busy place once the horses arrived, but at the moment it was empty except for a guy cutting the grass and Sherlock Holmes practicing his smoke rings.

I tiptoed up behind Sherlock and slapped him on the shoulder. "Hey, Sam Spade, long time no see!"

Sherlock immediately bent double and starting coughing like crazy. Like I was afraid he had swallowed his Merit Light. I continued to pat him on the back but it did no good. He was hunkered over and his face was turning blue. I found myself wondering if I give the kid a tracheotomy, how it will look with the lawyers: an act of mercy or an act of vengeance? I started feeling around in my pocket for my Swiss army knife. But after another minute his racket subsided and he straightened up.

"You surprised me," he said.

"Been smoking long?"

"About a month."

"It'll make your lungs turn black, then they'll flake apart just like old toast."

"That's what my mother says too." He looked worried for a moment. It made him look twenty-three instead of twenty-two. The front of his short blond hair curled forward like a cresting wave, but maybe it was just a depressed flattop

"How come you're following me?" I asked.

"Me?"

"You and that silly-looking Volkswagen."

"You saw me?"

"Give me a break. Who hired you?"

"I'm not at liberty to say." He looked proud to say that, as if there were some toughness in it. Standing this close to him, I thought his pink face was about the color and texture of barely chewed bubble gum. I figured he had to shave about once a month.

"You got a detective's license?" I asked.

A little cloud brushed across his forehead. "I only applied for it two weeks ago. I could show you the receipt."

"You mean you're tailing a guy and you don't even have a license?"

"Mr. Steinfeld said it would be all right."

Arnold Steinfeld was a lawyer representing one of my old ladies, Mrs. Florence Ross, who had once confided to me that she was related to Betsy Ross, the famous flagmaker. "She was your mother?" I had asked innocently. Unfortunately, my whimsical remark had gone unappreciated and it created a spot of cold air between us. As a result I wasn't surprised when Mrs. Ross started hollering for a lawyer when the crash came.

"So Steinfeld hired you?"

The kid blushed. "I'm not at liberty to say."

"What's your name?"

"Paul Butterworth."

"How come you decided to become a dick?"

"It was that or graduate school," said Butterworth, lowering his voice. "And my dad said I should do something with muscle in it. At Skidmore I was in English and creative writing." He gave me a bright smile.

I don't think of myself as having paternal feelings. Although I got a son in Chicago, he's forty and has a family to take care of him. But there was something about this Paul Butterworth that made me worry. I expect I would have worried for him no matter what he did for a living. Even if he milked cows, I'd worry that he might get kicked. Like I wanted to tell him, "Why don't you go home and read some good poems?" or "How about a nice glass of warm milk?"

"And what does Mr. Steinfeld want to find out about me?" I asked.

"I'm not at liberty to say." Butterworth smiled sheepishly. He was sorry to disappoint me. He didn't want to disappoint anybody but duty was duty and he had a job to perform.

"Look," I told him, "right now I'm off to the snack bar for a cup of regular and maybe a jelly doughnut. After that I got to hang around the paintings until eight o'clock. Then I'll be bicycling home by the usual route. But I promise not to go anywhere without telling you."

"I appreciate that, Mr. Plotz."

"Call me Vic," I said.

3

Sometimes Charlie Bradshaw would show up at the Pavilion to keep me company, although he had to pretend to be interested in the paintings so Ms. Fletcher wouldn't get mad. Charlie and me would stand in front of a painting of the English countryside and he would talk about Jesse James, his fantasy pal. He had been reading a book called *Jesse James: The Real Story,* which said that Jesse was not shot in the back of the head by Bob Ford in his little house in St. Joseph, Missouri, but that the whole thing had been a trick and that Jesse had supplied a stray body, then hung around as a pallbearer at his own funeral.

"There were at least a dozen guys who later claimed to be Jesse James," Charlie whispered. "But the thing is that Jesse had once accidentally shot off the tip of his left middle finger when cleaning his pistol back when he was riding with Bloody Bill Anderson. These guys who claimed to be Jesse all had regular hands."

"Do tell," I said.

So then I described how I spent the evening with the Queen of Softness. "First I cover her body with a mixture of cream and honey, then I lick it off and the cats lick it off too. It takes hours. . . ."

"I don't want to hear about it, Victor, I just don't want to hear about it."

In such a way are friendships solidified.

Sometimes we would go out and have a few words with Paul Butterworth. I'd told him that Charlie was a real detective and Butterworth kept asking for tips.

"And you don't carry your weapon all the time?" asked Butterworth. He had a way of nodding his head expectantly when asking a question.

"I only need it once in a blue moon," said Charlie.

"Jeez, I'm still waiting for them to approve my application to buy one. Getting the character witnesses was the hard part. I had to ask my creative writing teacher at Skidmore."

"That'll help," I said.

This first week at the Pavilion was pretty slow, but I got off on Saturday and Sunday and I took the Queen of Softness to the track. One day she wore a bright blue taffeta dress and the other a bright red taffeta dress. Both gave new meaning to the word "décolletage": a mixture of strawberry yogurt and vanilla pudding. On her driver's license the Queen of Softness gets called Rosemary Larkin and it says she is fifty-two. She runs a lunch counter on Route 29 between Saratoga and Schuylerville and she has a little place right behind it, a bungalow where she stores her hot tub and king-sized waterbed. As a hobby she sews brightly colored sequins and rhinestones on hats, neckties, blouses and vests and sells them at the lunch counter. Like she feels the world cannot have too many sequins and rhinestones.

Rosemary and I walk a lot at the track—more of a stroll— watching the jockeys weighing in, checking out the horses in the paddock and seeing that they get saddled properly, comparing them to what it says in the *Form,* hanging out near the finish line. It was sunny both days and Rosemary carried a parasol: blue on Saturday, red on Sunday. She is a big woman and she has a way of walking that parts the crowd in front of us just like Moses parted the Red Sea. On each day there must have been forty thousand people and they required a lot of parting.

Rosemary drives an old Ford Crown Victoria, which we took since she refused to ride on the handlebars of my Raleigh or to be seen in my Yugo. Paul Butterworth tagged along behind in his Beetle and followed us at the track. This wasn't as bad as it might have been because we could send him off to do things.

"Hey, Butterworth," I'd shout, "go get me a pretzel with double mustard!"

But because I was supposed to be broke, I couldn't bet and Rosemary had to bet for me. She uses a system where she combines the winningest jockey and the winningest trainer along with post position and her favorite colors and she always walks away with a couple of hundred bucks in her rhinestone purse.

Butterworth kept asking for tips.

"Because of my position as a financial adviser," I told him, "I find it morally equivocal to wager on the horses. Never have, never will."

The stands at Saratoga have been there since the 1860s: white on the outside, brown within and a brown shingled turret over the finish line where the gentleman of the track, Sonny Taylor, writes down the winners. A bunch of the two-year-olds running that day had been auctioned off across the street just the previous year, as had the three-year-olds, four-year-olds and so on. Now I realize that all the prettiness, all the flowers and sweet talk and fancy clothes, only exist to make the jerks cough up their bucks. But sometimes the illusion is so perfect—the horses being saddled in the paddock and the rich ladies in their gossamer dresses whispering a few words to the jockeys of their choice—that you almost believe in the magic, especially when the Queen of Softness has just made a bundle on the last race because the colors of the winning horse included her favorite shade of pink.

These are moments free of ugly consequences. No talk of lawyers, subpoenas, grand juries or jail time. But even though Paul Butterworth was growing on me, moderately, I couldn't help but see him as a representative of that real world which hoped to ensnare me in its chromium jaws. As Butterworth had confided in me, all his experience in taking creative writing courses at Skidmore was proving a great help when he wrote up his daily reports for Mr. Steinfeld. They had rhyme, they had meter and he made them zing. Even I, who am never speechless, was rendered nearly speechless.

And the next day, Monday, I pedaled back to the Pavilion, donned my brown uniform and looked stern at the occasional visitor who came to glom the paintings. Life at Fasig-Tipton was picking up. Tuesday, August 9th, the first day of the sale, was quickly approaching. The carpenters and gardeners and painters began working a little faster. More people showed up looking official. A few more Pinkertons could be seen wandering around the still-empty barns. A bartender started working, the snack bar took on an extra waitress. Then, the next week, the first yearlings began to arrive, along with a contingent of grooms, agents, owners, foremen, vets, horse reporters from *Bloodlines*—you name it. Sometimes a big farm, like Bridlewood Farm or White Oaks, would have a row of stalls with their names up on a sign, sometimes the stalls would go to an agent like Eaton-Williams or Dr. Jacques Levasseur from Quebec who would have horses from a bunch of smaller farms.

And signs started going up on the stable doors which would give the yearling's hip number and a description: roan colt, bay colt, chestnut colt, bay filly, and its date of birth in the winter or spring of '93, anywhere from January to June, although legally all the horses are born on January 1st. They give them a "hip" number not because the yearlings are cool in any way but because that is where they stick the little white piece of paper with the horse's number: right on the hipbone. It's the auction company that decides on the number, and it stands for where in the order of the sales the horse is going under the gavel.

These signs are on the inside of the stall doors, which are painted green and outlined in white. The doors are then pushed back against the outside wall so the signs face the eager deep-pocketed crowd. In place of the two-piece wooden stall door, the horse has a metal grill so the prospective buyer can take a peek at how his prospective piece of horseflesh is comporting himself. In the middle of the grill is a large white metal fan, because horses get hot and need their breezes. Between some of the stalls or at the ends of the rows are tack rooms and little offices and bunk rooms. All these farms or agents come with a lot of grooms—sometimes from the farm and sometimes hired locally—and a lot of people are are wandering about.

The grooms who work for a particular farm or agent usually have matching golf shirts: blue or red or green. And the agent or assistants or foremen tend to wear short-sleeved white shirts and khakis. Against the walls of the barn are director's chairs grouped in twos and threes, and the canvas backs and bottoms are the same color as the grooms' golf shirts: blue or red or green. Often suspended from the overhang of the roof are pots of red or pink geraniums. The overall appearance is of a place tremendously relaxed, but tremendously organized because in the three days of the yearling sales about twenty million smackers change hands and Fasig-Tipton gets five percent of it. You know how a person can appear cool on the outside but you realize he's full of jitters on the inside—that's how these horse people were.

During my break about four o'clock, I'd usually stroll around the grounds and Butterworth would stroll around about ten feet behind me. Seeing the barns and sales paddocks getting ready for the sales was like seeing a flower getting ready to blossom. By the end of the week, even though the horses were still arriving, you would start seeing folks in expensive clothes carrying little blue sales books which gave the particulars of all the horses. Taking a peek at one of these books, you'd see that some horses have a pretty active sex life. For instance there was Devil's Bag, born back in 1981, who had made $445,869 as a racehorse. He had then sired six crops of horses, 272 foals, 162 starters, 18 big winners, 106 lesser winners, and all these winners had brought in a total ten and a half million bucks. Doesn't 272 foals indicate an active sex life? Not bad for a thirteen-year-old. When I was that age I was still worrying about fur on my palms, warts on my fingers and other indications of onanism.

So a prospective buyer would check through the sales book and say to himself or herself, "Aha, here's a chestnut colt out of Criminal Type and Tadorna. I must take a gander at that." And he'd stroll over and ask one of the grooms to bring Hip Thirty-five or Eighty-six or One Eighty-one out of its stall and parade it around as he took notes on his pad.

Well, I liked that. I liked it so much I took to doing it myself. You see, I missed being a man of money. I missed being deferred to. So the second week, which was less than a week away from the beginning of the auction, I started coming to the sales paddocks an hour or two earlier than necessary and I'd wear my suit: a dove-gray summer-weight with a vest. And sometimes I would wear a fedora.

I'd wander through the sales paddock looking like a buyer, and each day I added a little to my costume. Hung binoculars around my neck, carried the *Racing Form*. I'd stroll up to a stall, ogle the sign and say, "Aha, bay filly out of Houston and Redeemer. . . . I'd like to take a look at that."

Then the head groom or even the agent would bring out the horse and walk it back and forth, while I watched how its feet moved and what its hips were doing.

Sometimes I'd say to the agent, "Toes in a little bit, don't you think?"

And he'd say, "Oh, sir, I don't believe so."

Or I'd say, "That right back knee looks a trifle swollen."

And he'd say, "Everything's perfect, sir. Would you like to see the x-rays?"

I'd look at the horse's teeth and have the groom lift up all four of the horse's feet and I'd tap the horse's ribs as if sounding him for tuberculosis.

"How come he hangs his head so low?" I'd ask. "Is he depressed?"

Or, if the horse had two white front stockings, I'd say, "I've always heard that two front stockings brought bad luck."

Or maybe I'd make up a disease. "Have you had this horse tested for scabrax?"

"I beg your pardon, sir?"

"Scabrax. The horse's belly turns to glass and breaks into a million pieces."

"I don't believe I've heard of that, sir."

"And how long have you been doing this, boy?"

Well, I can't tell you how much pleasure these harmless impersonations gave me. In no time, I'd have a crowd of half a dozen grooms, foremen, agents and owners bowing and scraping and sweating by the bucket. I'd keep this up for half an hour until I had a dozen of them singing, "No, sir! Yes, sir!" as if in a church choir as the horse kept walking back and forth looking at me with its big brown innocent eyes.

And of course Paul Butterworth would follow me from barn to barn. He disapproved of my behavior and would stand to the side shaking his head. So then I started pretending that he was the guy with the big bucks and I was just an intermediary. The agent would be jumping through hoops around some yearling and I'd turn to Butterworth and say, "You notice that film on the right eye, sir?" And Butterworth would blush, which would make the agent go absolutely crazy with nervousness and despair.

"A finer pair of eyes has never been seen on a living horse!" the agent would squeak.

One of my pleasures came from the fact that the number one rule around horse barns is Don't Rile the Horses. Horses must be made to think the world is sweet and gentle, otherwise they get upset. So there I'd be, turning the crank, as it were, saying, "That's a funny bend in the horse's tail," or "Teeth look small, don't you think?" and these grooms or agents or owners would want to pull their hair and scream but of course they couldn't scream because that would upset the poor horse. They couldn't even hiss. So they would lock their mouths tight shut and their cheeks would get bigger and bigger just like a balloon getting ready to bust and then they might whisper, "Do you really believe so, sir? Looks fine to me, sir."

Then I'd turn to Butterworth and say, "It's a shame about this colt's fetlocks," and the agent or whoever would get redder and redder.

Oh, it was a pleasure.

Now and then of course, I'd push the whole charade a trifle too far and the agent would draw himself up and say, "I'd like to see your credentials, sir."

Then I'd turn to Butterworth and ask deferentially, "Would you mind if he took a peek at your ID?"

And Butterworth, thinking I meant his detective license, would say, "I'm afraid I've only got the receipt."

You might think I knew absolutely zip about how a horse should look, but my brief acquaintance with the bronze bust of Humphrey S. Finney had led me to look up his autobiography, *Fair Exchange,* in which he gave a lot of good advice. For instance:

A normal foot is neither too steep nor too wide and flat. About a 45-degree slope from a good rounded toe and with good wide

heels is what you want. A flat foot is often found in horses imported from the European countries where young horses are
usually out in lush wet grazing. It takes quite a time to get the
average imported animal's feet in good shape for American racing. The foot should hit the ground fair and square, neither side
being higher or lower than the other, and the frog should have
contact with the ground. A brittle, shelly foot is a curse often
found. And there's no doubt that white feet do have a tendency
to be softer than dark ones. A tough black foot is most desirable.

The book contained much useful information of this nature,
and I loved to pick up a horse's hoof, shake my head at the agent
and say, "Too much lush wet grazing."

Mr. Finney even had a little poem.

> *One white foot, ride him for your life*
> *Two white feet, give him to your wife,*
> *Three white feet, send him far away,*
> *Four white feet, keep him not a day.*

I'd quote this poem to some saddened agent and he'd squeak,
"Secretariat had three white feet, three very fast white feet."

Unfortunately, the number of sellers was limited and after a
few days I had interacted with quite a few. Also there was the
problem of my position as guardian of valuable paintings. Three
or four times when I was working, an agent or owner whose life
I had made miserable would show up in the balcony of the Pavilion hoping to buy a nice equine head for his den. He would
look at me, then look away, then look again.

"Don't I know you from someplace?" he would ask.

I would be wearing my uniform by that time and I'd try to
yank my cap down over my brow. "I don't believe so, sir," I

would respond, keeping my face somewhat averted as the fellow struggled to take a better look.

"Weren't you asking my man to show you the bay colt?"

"Oh, no, sir, I'm deathly afraid of horses."

Well, I was never entirely believed and I could see that my innocent folderol about being a rich buyer was coming to an end. But on the Friday before the sale was to start a batch of ten stalls were suddenly filled by an agent from Kentucky by the name of Henry O'Leary. Late that morning I strolled by in my three-piece dove-gray suit. Two grooms, hardly out of their teens, were brushing a nice-looking chestnut colt with a white left front stocking and a white blaze on his forehead. I paused and eyed the horse nose to nose. The colt snorted and pulled back.

"Walk this fellow around for me, will you, boy?"

The younger of the two grooms took hold of the bridle and led the colt down the line of stalls, turned around and came back. He was a nice little colt, somewhat shy, a little nervous, darting quick glances at the horses in the other stalls, making soft flatulent noises with his upper lip.

"Limps a little, doesn't he?"

"I don't believe so, sir," said the kid. Both he and the other groom were wearing khakis and purple golfing shirts.

"What about scabrax—has he been tested?"

"He's been x-rayed and scoped for everything you can imagine." The boy walked him back and forth again and when he returned I stopped them and looked in the colt's mouth.

"Teeth seem small," I said. "He must be off his feed." I patted the colt lightly on the neck. About ten feet away I noticed Paul Butterworth looking embarrassed.

"They may be small, sir, but they bite," said the groom.

"And what do you mean by that?" I asked.

I had turned half away and in that moment the colt leaned

forward and solidly nipped my left buttock. It was one of those occasions when I climbed high in the air yet lacked a ladder. The teeth hurt and I soared up several feet.

"Yeow!" I said.

"Seem sharp enough for you, sir?" asked the groom.

And that was how I met Fleshpot, otherwise known as Hip Fifty-seven.

4

I was still standing there rubbing my backside when a youngish fellow in a white short-sleeved shirt came out of an office next to the stall. He had straight black hair that hung in bangs all around his head, like Prince Valiant or maybe Moe in the Three Stooges. Like a good-sized bowl had been placed over his head and whatever stuck out got cut off.

"Hey," he said to the groom with a certain amount of scorn, "this guy's a security guard over at the Pavilion. He's been going around pretending to be a buyer."

"Trick or treat," I said.

The two young grooms and the guy with the Three Stooges haircut looked at me appraisingly. At that moment the horse tried to take another taste of my backside, but I jumped away.

"What's with your horse?" I asked, recovering my balance.

"He's just friendly," said one of the grooms.

"He tries to do that to all of us," said the other.

"Fleshpot," I said. "He's probably oversexed."

"Why don't you beat it," said the guy with the haircut, "or I'll grab a Pinkerton."

So that put an end to my harmless impersonations, which suited Butterworth just as well because he found them a trial. Mostly he would stand about fifteen feet away, squinching his eyes, afraid I would drag him into it.

"How can you do that sort of thing?" he asked as we walked back to the Pavilion. He was taller than me by about five inches and I kept glancing at his plaid-covered shoulder.

"I was born with an irrepressible nature," I told him, "and it's gets more irrepressible by the year." But that wasn't quite true. I only started changing after my wife died, but that was over thirty years ago. Until then I had obeyed all the rules, brushed my teeth three times a day and washed my hands every time I took a leak.

That Friday Ms. Fletcher hired another guard and changed my hours, bringing me in on Sunday and having me start at two on Monday afternoon, then work from four to midnight on the three days of the sales. I didn't see much of the other guard, but he was a seedy cuss moping his way out of middle age toward the darker side of life: big belly and going bald. If someone had tried to swipe a painting off him, he would probably give up the ghost. Too bad Ms. Fletcher couldn't get another guard like me: someone in the prime of life.

I spent much of the weekend at the track with the Queen of Softness with Butterworth tagging along behind. A perfect August weekend, not too hot and no rain. Before we went I gave Rosemary some bucks so Butterworth wouldn't see me spending my own money, but would think Rosemary was treating me. Once I even tried to touch Butterworth for a double sawbuck.

"Twenty bucks," I told him. "I got a tip on a fantastic horse in the fifth. Rubber Mother, a sure winner. I'll make it back in spades." We were standing by the paddock watching the horses being saddled. I had left Rosemary at a table in the clubhouse sipping a mimosa.

"Mr. Steinfeld said I shouldn't even talk to you anymore," said Butterworth.

"Give me twenty bucks and I'll give you back fifty in under an hour."

"I thought you didn't bet." He raised one of his eyebrows as if he believed he had made an important discovery.

"But this is a sure thing. Look, give me twenty and I'll give you back a hundred. I can't do better than that."

"A hundred?"

"Sure, that's half of what I'll make myself."

"I don't know." Butterworth had one of those faces that always looked fretful, like a dog that can't remember where it put a bone.

"What're are you scared of? You don't like money or something? You rich?"

"I only have twenty-five bucks to my name."

"Well, now you have one hundred and five. Jesus, Butterworth, get real."

So the long and the short of it was that he gave me the double sawbuck and I lost it. Rubber Mother, a three-year-old gelding, didn't even show.

"No balls," I told Butterworth. "I thought it'd make him run faster, you know? Less weight in the hindquarters."

Butterworth looked pretty gloomy about this and his flattop sagged. Unfortunately, I told the Queen of Softness, thinking she would appreciate the humor, and she gave Butterworth twenty bucks. "Never give Vic money," she told Butterworth. "He's not to be trusted."

"Whose side are you on?" I asked Rosemary.

On Sunday before work, I escorted Rosemary around the sales paddock to see the yearlings. A lot of the grooms and agents recognized me as the doofus who had made their pet colt or filly jump through hoops, and I got a lot of scowls.

"You don't seem too popular," Rosemary told me.

"They envy me for being with such a pretty lady."

I took her by Fleshpot's stall and the two young grooms were giving the chestnut colt a good brushing. Even while being brushed, Fleshpot would try to nip their asses.

"Watch out!" said one.

"Here he comes again," said the other.

They were cousins and lived down near Kingston. They said they had been hired for just these two weeks, but that they often worked as grooms down at Belmont and Aqueduct, taking the train into the city. The older one was twenty and his name was Harry Macklin. The other was Rolf Macklin and he was eighteen. They were both big strapping black-haired guys who blushed and tried not to look at the décolletage when the Queen of Softness chatted with them.

"So you both just met this horse?" she asked.

"Just in the past week, ma'am," said Harry. "Watch out, ma'am, he'll nip anyone."

Rosemary lightly tapped Fleshpot on the tip of his nose with her parasol and the horse snorted. "He's a dear," she said. "What are those calluses on the inside of his knees?"

"They're called nighteyes, ma'am," said Rolf.

"Or chestnuts," said Harry.

"They're the fingerprints of the horse," I added just to retain some influence over the conversation. "In New York State they photograph them. If a horse gets swapped for a ringer, they can tell by comparing photos of the nighteyes. Actually, they're a residual finger. The prehistoric horse probably swung from the trees with them."

"I thought they put tattoos on their lower lips," said Rosemary.

"They only do that when they start racing," I said. "These yearlings don't have tattoos. See?" I pulled down Fleshpot's lower lip. It was as pink and unblemished as a baby's cheek. "They got lots of ways to identify the horses. For instance, when the vets test a horse's blood, they look for forty-eight different factors."

Throughout my learned disquisition the two cousins looked uncomfortable. I assumed they disliked my parading around all this insider knowledge, but I had only picked it up the day before so I really didn't think it mine.

"How much do you expect this horse to sell for?" Rosemary asked the cousins.

"He's got good blood," said Rolf. "The boss is expecting to make a lot of money."

"His granddaddy was Seattle Slew," said Harry. "And he's got Secretariat and Garden Party on his dam's side."

"And he was personally blessed by Pope John Paul," I said.

"I didn't know that," said Rolf.

At that moment Fleshpot tried to nip me again but like a bunny I hopped away.

Now that the auction was almost upon us more people were showing up to glom the paintings and Ms. Fletcher even sold a few, at least little red "sold" stickers appeared next to some, although Ms. Fletcher might have put them up just to increase excitement. She was a sneaky cuss. I got to make harrumphing noises behind a lot of people and make them jump. I mean, most people have a residual reservoir of guilt and you only have to know how to tap into it to make them blanch and hurry away. Several times Ms. Fletcher suggested that I try to call less attention to myself. The temptation to give her a snappy reply was almost impossible to resist, but, as I say, I couldn't afford to lose the job and so I stayed deferentialish. It was only outside the Pavilion that I carried on, probably in reaction to being so good inside.

"Do you know where I can find Smother's painting of Lord Toedrop winning at Essex?" asked an elderly gentleman.

"I'm sorry, sir," I said. "Ms. Fletcher says I'm not to exchange words with the gentry. You'll have to speak with her."

Remarks like that were about all the fun I could have. Pathetic, wasn't it.

Monday night before the sales I went over to Charlie Bradshaw's cottage on the lake after work. It was about ten-thirty by the time I got there, and I caught him reading a book.

"So tomorrow's the big day," he said. He must have been getting ready to go to bed because he was already wearing his slippers and blue terry-cloth bathrobe. And his hair was combed, Charlie always combs his hair before going to bed.

"Are you coming over to watch? I can let you into the Pavilion." I had made myself a Jack Daniel's Manhattan and stood in the kitchen doorway. His place only has three rooms: big living room with a fieldstone fireplace, kitchen and bedroom. Out the back the lake was doing whatever lakes do in the still of the night: lapping and sloshing. Charlie has a dock poking into the water and he likes to sit at the end and watch the fish jump.

"I've got to be over at the backstretch. Someone's been stealing stuff from the offices. They've lost two computers."

"And the Pinkertons can't catch them?"

"I guess not." Charlie smiled. He can't stand the Pinkertons because they made Jesse James's life such a misery and killed his retarded stepbrother.

"So you'll just hang out?"

"Yup. Actually, it's a nuisance because I had to break a date with Janey, but I need the money."

"How are you and Janey doing?"

Charlie sighed and glanced out at the lake. "She wants me to move into her place in town and I don't want to give up the cottage. Jesus, Victor, she's got three teenage daughters! I love them, but each has her own stereo and they play them as loud as they can, trying to drown out the others.''

"I guess they don't play much Guy Lombardo.''

"You ever heard of hip-hop?''

"Bunny music?'' I asked.

"Not exactly. I'd hate to get myself so worked up that I yelled at them.''

"So what're you going to do?''

"Janey says I've got to make up my mind. Either make a serious commitment or stop coming over.''

"The big ultimatum,'' I said.

"I don't see why things can't just stay the same.''

"Change, Charlie, that's what life is all about.''

Charlie gave me a glance that suggested that he disliked being patronized. By this time I was sitting on the couch while he sat in the armchair by the fireplace. On the walls were framed photographs of Willie Sutton, John Dillinger and Pretty Boy Floyd. Friendly guys who filled Charlie with good cheer.

"Doesn't Rosemary ever ask you about your future intentions?'' asked Charlie.

"She's a one-day-at-a-time kind of lady. The future's too iffy a proposition.''

"Janey says it's just because the future is an iffy proposition that we should stabilize the relationship.''

"Sounds like being sunk in concrete.''

"What are you going to do after the yearling sales?''

"The exhibit runs through next week. Then, if the lawyers are still after me, maybe I'll go out to Chicago and see my son, although it'll mean sleeping on the couch, putting up with his kids and eating kosher. Have you heard anything about whether they're going to press charges on me?''

"You might get a civil suit. You have a lawyer?''

"Yeah, but he costs me and arm and a leg. Maybe I could defend myself.''

"I guess life in the fast lane has its drawbacks."

"This is just a pothole, Charlie. Even in a civil suit they can't prove I have any extra bucks. This old lady Ross is just being spiteful. She wanted some stock so I bought her some stock. Can I help it if the stock market did a loop the loop?"

"How come no one else lost their shirt?"

"Hog bellies can be a treacherous enterprise, Charlie. If I explained the ins and outs it would take all night. Just accept the fact that there was a glitch and all my money drained away."

"I wonder who's driving your Mercedes now?" asked Charlie.

In such a way did we pass the evening. A few drinks, a little chitchat. The next day the yearling sales would begin. August was winding its way down its little path. Somewhere far to the north the winter storms were preparing themselves. Charlie's windows facing the lake were open and now and then I could hear the cry of a loon: that mournful warble. Demented and passionate. It's wonderful in this life how at any moment we assume what tomorrow will be like and the day after and the day after that. How often doesn't it work out like that? When I got up to make myself another drink, I saw the dim shape of Paul Butterworth's Volkswagen Beetle parked out on the side of the road with the light on inside. I once asked him what he did standing outside the Pavilion all afternoon and he looked uncomfortable and said he read poetry. Then he quoted a few lines from a book he had with him.

> He hates to wake up in the morning alone,
> What it's like to squeeze juice for one,
> To stumble around in only pajama bottoms
> With no one to admire his recent tan
> Or explicate his significant dreams.

So I figured that was what he was doing sitting out in his Beetle late that Monday night as he waited for me to go home:

reading poetry. What were his future plans? What dumb idea had led him to decide to be a private investigator? But tomorrow the yearling sales would being. Lots of action and excitement. All the pomp and pageantry that rich folks require when they spend their big bucks. And Murder with a capital M, it would be the last thing on anyone's mind, or almost anyone.

5

———————
———————
———————

Let me describe one guy's job to you. You got a Pavilion full of rich people clutching their blue guides to the yearling sales and all with their little horse-buying agendas. Lots of them have portable phones and they are talking to their buyers in Japan, California, you name it. A lot of the ladies are dressed in top-dollar items. For instance, Mrs. Whitney is sitting down in the front row and the pretty pastel dress covering her *cuerpo* would pay for a horse's upkeep for an entire year.

The auction ring is a U-shaped area covered with green saw-dust, which isn't really sawdust, and it is separated from the front row of red seats by a barrier consisting of two thick white ropes supported by little metal black posts each topped by a horse's head. Facing the audience are four spotters working for Fasig-Tipton, four men in evening dress who pick up the bids, because let me tell you, these men and women who bid on the horses are nothing if not subtle. If I was going to bid a hundred grand on an adolescent nag that has done nothing but eat and poop for the past year and a half, I would jump up and down and wave my arms. But these rich folks are different. They lift a little finger or raise an eyebrow and the spotter who spots them shouts, "Yo!" or something like that, and the lighted number on the scoreboard pops up another five or ten grand. There are two more spotters standing up in the press box covering the balcony and there is even a spotter outside with the hoi polloi, and they are all wired in to the auctioneer and the announcer, who stand in the pulpit at the back of the U-shaped auction ring. The auctioneer has a nice southern accent to show he's from Kentucky, where the best horses come from. The announcer has a nice British accent to show he's from England, where the best money comes from. Now and then when the bidding lags, the announcer interrupts the auctioneer, by saying, "Ladies and gentlemen, I would like to repeat that this bay colt was sired by Danzig, sire of ten crops of winners totaling earnings of thirty-two and a quarter million dollars. Sire of champions like Dance Smartly, Chief's Crown and Pine Bluff. This is one of the prettiest pieces of horseflesh that we will see all evening." Then the bidding picks up again and the spotters go back to shouting "Yo!" as the auctioneer calls out: "Eighty, eighty, eighty, do I hear ninety?"

You might think I have forgotten about this guy's job that I was going to describe to you, but I haven't. In about a four-hour period they go through sixty horses, which means they are selling a horse about every four minutes. And these horses are all lined up out back: one in the chute, maybe three or four in the walking ring, maybe two or three in another walking ring, several more are being led through the crowd by a Pinkerton and a groom with the Pinkerton saying, "Watch your back," and, of course, the horses that have been sold are being led back to their stalls usually without a Pinkerton. This is a lot of movement and there are probably three or four hundred people in the paddock area, a lot of them at the bar but also lots of people just glomming the horses: some of them are buyers, most of them are wishful thinkers.

But there is a moment of fateful transition when the yearling is moved from the relative quiet of the chute into the auction ring inside of the Pavilion. Like I say, the horses have to be kept calm, but it is hard to transfer a horse from the soothing dark to bright lights, the auctioneer's noisy prattle, the shouted "Yo!"'s of the spotters and the stares of several hundred well-dressed rich people without the horse becoming suddenly anxious. And what does a horse do when he gets anxious? He whinnies, sure. He rears up, of course. He tries to get away, you bet. But the main thing he does, which requires that one fellow's expertise, is to take a dump. The horse is led into the auction ring, sees all the commotion and immediately unloads: one, two, three. At which point a black guy dressed up like a Pullman waiter hurries out with a broom and dustpan and makes the green pseudo-sawdust tidy again. Now how would you like to have that on your résumé? Dump-keeper. Poop-scooper.

So this was how it was. No matter how chagrined I felt about wearing a silly brown uniform and guarding a bunch of silly paintings, at least I wasn't sweeping up horse caca about five feet from the expensively stylish shoes of Mrs. Whitney. Isn't this one of life's intrinsic truths? No matter how bad things become, there's always something to feel good about.

But I'll bet this dump-keeper, this poop-scooper, got health insurance. Probably it was even a skilled profession, because he swept up the golden nuggets from under the yearling's nervous hooves with the aplomb of a sommelier removing the cork from a bottle of Dom Pérignon. I bet there isn't a job on earth that doesn't have some pride that goes along with it. And when the dump-keeper returned to the arms of his loving wife that evening, he would brag: "I scooped up some real golden nuggets tonight."

Around nine-thirty I got a break from my paintings and I wandered out into the paddock area. Butterworth picked me up and trailed about ten feet behind me in his nonchalant foot-stumbling way. The whole place was crowded with people watching the show inside the Pavilion through the big windows or eyeing the horses in the walking ring or just ambling around. The bar was packed. I wandered back toward the barns where there were fewer people. By now about forty horses had been sold and their stalls were shut up. Ownership of the yearlings changed to the buyer with the fall of the hammer, but the yearling wasn't transferred to the buyer's possession until he got a stable release. The horses still to be auctioned that night were getting nicely brushed. Their heads and legs were rubbed down with baby oil and a kind of colorless nail polish was put on their hooves to make them shine.

I walked back to check on Fleshpot. Rolf Macklin was brushing his tail and his cousin Harry was brushing his mane. They seemed nervous and when they took a glance at me it wasn't with the happiness that I like to see on a youngster's face. Fleshpot's fur shone nicely, and when he saw me, he gave me a whinny. I started to pat his head.

"Don't touch him," said Rolf. "You'll get oil on your hands."

The two grooms seemed alone.

"Have you sold any of your horses yet?" I asked.

"This'll be the first," said Harry. "The others will go tomorrow."

"Good luck," I said. As I turned away, Fleshpot leaned forward to nip my backside but I was too quick for him. "You better warn the new owner about his unfortunate habits," I added.

Rolf didn't say anything. Harry nodded. They were busy guys and their big moment was coming. I walked around the paddock, talking to a few of the grooms and agents. Some of their horses had come in under what they had expected, some over, and some had been buy-backs, which is when an agent buys back his own horse because it's not bringing in the bucks that he thinks he can get for it someplace else. Butterworth tailed along behind and sometimes he would exchange a word with a groom as well. I realized that he had been making various acquaintances at the track and even when he was supposed to be following me, he would give some guy a wave or say howdy-do. It was a warm night and the moon was just two days past full. Now and then I caught a glimpse of it hanging over the Oklahoma Track, a little lopsided but bright and shiny nonetheless.

Sometimes I stretched my half-hour lunch break to forty-five minutes, but on this night I made sure to be back inside by the time that Fleshpot or Hip Fifty-seven came under the gavel. It was about eleven-thirty and the Pavilion wasn't as crowded as it had been earlier in the evening.

"Ladies and gentlemen," said the British announcer, "we are proud to offer you tonight a very nice chestnut colt out of Woodman and Affirmatively. Rarely have we had a colt with such illustrious lineage. The second sire was Seattle Slew. The second dam, Garden Party, was covered by Secretariat."

He want on like that for a while and the auctioneer started the bidding at one hundred thousand. Fleshpot stood calmly as his bridle was held by a guy in a white jacket. Now and then he raised or lowered his head as if in response to the bidding. The white blaze on his forehead glistened in the overhead lights.

As for the bidding, there seemed to be about a dozen people who hoped to take Fleshpot home with them. The spotters kept shouting out "Yo!" or "Hep!" and the price went up to one-forty, one-sixty, one-eighty, two hundred. I scanned the crowd to see who was doing the bidding but I only could pick out one old guy toward the front who had his reading glasses folded into a wand and when he wanted to up the ante he would make a little circle with his glasses in the air. The price went over two hundred thousand and a couple of hopeful buyers dropped out.

The spotters all had little relationships going with the active bidders, giving them winks, grins and philosophic shrugs. Now and then the announcer would stop the bidding to crank up the crowd a bit more.

"I want to remind you, ladies and gentlemen, that Woodman was the sire of eight black type winners including Hansel, a three-million-dollar champion and winner of the Belmont Stakes and the Preakness . . ."

Then some of the bidders who had fallen by the wayside came back again and in no time the price had risen to four hundred thousand. Now the process got a little slower. The prospective buyers were thinking long and deeply. I was able to pick out two of the bidders and both were talking frantically into portable phones, presumably not to each other.

"Ladies and gentlemen," said the auctioneer in his drawl, "I have four-ten, do I hear four-twenty? No? Four-ten going once . . ."

"Hep!" shouted a spotter.

"Four-twenty. Do I hear four-thirty?"

"Mr. Sullivan, do you think your party wants four-thirty?" The Brit would say this as if he wondered if Mr. Sullivan's party might want a cup of tea.

And the spotter, Mr. Sullivan, would make an inquiring gesture to some guy in a lilac suit who was jabbering into a phone. Then he would nod and Mr. Sullivan would shout, "Yo!"

"Four-thirty, do I hear four-forty? What about your party, Mr. White . . ."

"Hep!"

"Four-forty, do I hear four-fifty?"

And so it went. A lot of people were watching through the windows, because every word said by the auctioneer or the Brit was also being broadcast outside. By this time there was no other noise in the Pavilion except for Fleshpot, who gave a whinny.

You know that kind of silence that is so silent as to be almost noisy, as if everyone was holding their breath at once? That's how it was. The bidding crept up to five hundred thousand and hovered there. The auctioneer's drawl got a little slower. The Brit was standing with his hands over his tummy as if he were digesting something big and sweet.

"Do I hear five-ten?" asked the auctioneer. "Mr. Sullivan? Mr White? What about you, Mr. Edwards?"

"Hep!"

"All right, five-twenty. Shall we go higher, gentlemen?"

The auctioneer cranked it up to five-thirty, but that was that. People began talking like crazy and there was a rush of sound. Fleshpot took this opportunity to nip his handler's backside, and the man rose up nearly as high as the auctioneer's pulpit. Around the Pavilion were other Fasig-Tipton employees in evening dress with little sales contracts and several of these were closing in on a lean-looking fellow who looked rather red in the face. Personally, if I had just spent five hundred and thirty thousand dollars, I would be pale.

Although this was the biggest sale of the night and bigger than any sale the previous year, it was well under the record of four point six million spent for a chestnut colt out of Northern Dancer and Bubbling in 1984. But the mid-eighties were the fat years and the early nineties were the thin ones. Back in 1985, Fasig-Tipton grossed nearly fifty-one million on 196 yearlings at Saratoga, while this year they would be tickled pink to gross twenty million.

The guy handling Fleshpot rubbed his bottom and got a good grip on the horse's bridle as he prepared to lead him out the back and turn him over to either Harry or Rolf. Already Hip Fifty-eight was getting ready to enter the ring. Fleshpot's big five minutes were over.

I ambled quickly over to the stairs, meaning to get outside and follow Fleshpot back to his stall. You know how you feel proud when a pal does well? That's how I felt about Fleshpot, and I wanted to rub his greasy snout. That money, more than half a million, was probably more than I had earned in my entire life. The horse was a celebrity and I felt honored that he had had my backside clenched between his front teeth.

There were still a lot of people outside, despite the hour. Probably a couple of hundred with many over at the bar. Maybe there were five or six more horses to be auctioned that night, then the Fasig-Tipton guys would count up their bucks, offer a little press conference to the horse reporters, then head over to the Wishing Well, where they did their serious late-night drinking. I walked after Fleshpot, who was quartered in Barn Three West. Because of the crowd, I lost sight of him. People in the business of surveying horseflesh walk pretty slowly and I kept getting stuck behind the browsers. I glanced around and there was Paul Butterworth ambling after me. He had dressed appropriately for the evening—dark blue blazer, khaki pants, white shirt, red, blue and purple striped tie.

I was just passing the first barns on my right with the Fasig-Tipton sales offices on my left when I heard shouting farther ahead. This quickly degenerated into a yelling and screaming with more shouts and the sound of a high whinny. People stopped and turned toward the ruckus. Several Pinkertons ran past, then some official types in dark suits. I began to move a little faster. Suddenly the thirty or so people in front of me began running to the sides or back toward me. Again I heard a whinny and a scream. As the crowd divided I saw a black horse galloping toward me. Maybe it was a colt, maybe a filly. I didn't pause to check but ran for the wall of the barn on my right, where I flattened myself, thinking that I didn't flatten as well as I used to.

The horse galloped by, although perhaps "gallop" is the wrong word. It bucked, hopped, skipped and kicked. It ran sideways. It stood up on its hind legs and staggered along. Back in June when the New York Ballet ballerinas did this, people cheered. When a horse does it, people screech and run for cover. The horse went past me in no time, pausing only to bounce against a poky fellow who didn't jump out of the way fast enough. The poky fellow was body-checked about ten feet. There were a dozen other horses within view and their grooms or owners or agents rushed to get them under cover.

At one moment this had been sedate city, now it was a roller coaster. The black horse hopped a fence, tore across the grass toward the bar, knocked over some chairs, banged into another person: this time a groom who was trying to lay hands on him. Lots of people were running away from the horse, lots of people were running toward him. I was one of the latter because I wanted to see what would happen next. Several people were lying on the ground groaning as nervous Fasig-Tipton flunkies leaned over them. The black horse leapt another fence, then rushed back toward me and about a dozen other anxious folks. I got behind a tree. A lady who was a little slower got bumped into the tree, a fidgety adolescent maple. She lay on her back and wheezed. She was about forty-five and wore a maroon dress that was now up above her knees. Her eyes were wide open as if she was doing a silent inventory of all her bones. The black horse was leaping around about fifteen feet away. First it would dance right, then it would dance left. Like it was terrified and no one else was happy either. Chaos, as they say, reigned supreme.

I crouched down by the lady who had gotten bumped. "Anything broken?" I asked.

"I don't think so." She gave me a brave smile that was a trifle crooked.

I dragged her over behind the tree, then looked to see what the horse was doing. It was galloping by the Pavilion. It would stop, rear up, then tear off in another direction, stop and rear up again, then take off again. About twenty grooms and private coppers were trying to box it in by the walking ring. I looked around for Butterworth but didn't see him. The black horse turned and charged the grooms and coppers. One kid tried to grab the horse's bridle but he got knocked aside. The horse came galloping back toward me and the lady who was still lying on the ground. I got in front of her, then took off my brown cap and shook it at the horse: "Whoosh! Whoosh!"

I don't think the horse noticed my endeavors but when it passed again I saw he was a colt. People were shouting and running every which way, but more and more grooms and coppers and Fasig-Tipton types were trying to box the horse in against one of the barns or against a fence or a wall. Several grooms ran by with some kind of portable fence. I left the lady by the tree and hurried after them.

By now the black colt was in the southwest corner of the paddock between two barns and the blacksmith shop. A bunch of guys making their way toward him had ropes. When the horse had rushed past me the last time I had seen that his shins were bleeding from where he had taken a clunk when jumping a barrier. He was getting to be one tired animal, and I believe he was thinking twice about the horrors of being caught. He stood shivering and puffing with his eyes rolling around in his big black head. The guys with the portable fences moved slowly toward him. Then someone tossed a rope around his neck, then came another. The black colt bucked and tried to rear up. A vet pushed forward and gave him a shot of something. The horse gave a loud whinny, a kind of I-don't-like-any-of-this! whinny. A few more ropes were put around his neck and a blanket over his back. A groom covered the colt's eyes with a blindfold and he began to settle down.

I walked back toward the Pavilion. Maybe the colt had injured half a dozen folks, maybe more. It wasn't out of malice.

They were just in the way. This rushing around had just been a bad life decision on the colt's part: a good idea that turned out to be a bad idea. We all make them. By now I heard sirens, ambulances most likely. I waited until they arrived and watched some people get loaded onto stretchers, including the lady in the maroon dress who I had dragged out of the way. She gave me a little wave. I glanced around for Butterworth but didn't see him. After about fifteen minutes I took a walk over to Fleshpot's stall to see how the chestnut colt was doing. When I got there, I found everything shut up for the night. The grooms were gone. Fleshpot stood at the back of his stall, facing the wall as if he were reading something printed upon it. I congratulated him on his sale price but he didn't even cock an ear at me.

6

The next day as I bicycled over to the Humphrey S. Finney Pavilion around three o'clock I felt a strange and mysterious lack. After two blocks I realized what it was. Paul Butterworth was not doodling along behind me in his lime-green Beetle. He had not followed me home the previous night either, but then I had figured we had missed each other in the hoopla surrounding the hysterical black colt which had tried to race fifteen Kentucky Derbies all at once within the sales paddock.

Although I had tolerably liked Butterworth, his absence struck me as a sign of liberation, and I rang my little bell. It indicated that Lawyer Arnold Steinfeld had pulled him off the job and presumably he had done so because he realized he didn't have a legal leg to stand on, which meant that in only a few days I could rejoin the fast lane and stop being humble. I rang my bell again and swerved the old Raleigh at a marmalade cat which scampered out of the way.

Just that morning I had seen my own lawyer, Arthur Woodward, and it was his opinion that if Steinfeld hadn't filed papers by now, then he probably didn't have a case.

"What Arnold Steinfeld is doing is no more than harassment," Woodward had told me.

"Absolutely shameful," I answered.

"You're just going to have to hang in there, Victor."

"Call me Vic," I said.

But this afternoon it seemed that my hanging-in-there days were nearly done. Butterworth had been removed from the case and from now on I could drive to work if I wanted to. I could take a limousine. I considered looking up Butterworth later that evening to have a drink and celebrate. To tell the truth, all this bicycling had removed from my *cuerpo* a couple of pounds which I hated to see go. Diminishment, how can people stand it?

When I got to the sales paddocks, I parked my bike back by a bunkhouse and proceeded to wander past the barns and eyeball the livestock. A few of the horses which had been auctioned the previous evening had already been shipped away, and their stalls were closed up tight. Maybe one hundred and fifty people were strolling around the paddock area. There was a certain buzz which I guessed was because of the horse running loose last night and causing all that commotion. The *Saratogian* had said that seven people had been injured. Most had been simply bruised but two had broken bones: a groom had busted some ribs when he had been banged into a tree and a lady had gotten her leg broken.

The black colt had apparently been made jittery by all the people and had broken away from his groom. He was due to be auctioned on Thursday, and his owner, Cottonwood Farms, still hadn't decided to scratch him or let him go under the hammer. I thought it would be a pretty sight for the colt to get loose in the Pavilion and gallop up and down the aisles. The colt had sustained bruises and cuts on his shins, but the owner said they weren't serious. Like what else could he say? Wasn't he hoping to sell the colt for a big bundle? Fasig-Tipton officials were full of apology and the reporter said that two dozen long-stemmed red roses had been sent to the lady who had had her leg broke, which I thought must have been nice for her.

I had a mild desire to say goodbye to Fleshpot before he was shipped off to his new owners and I was idly strolling in the direction of his barn. The *Saratogian* had covered the sale the previous evening and had given Fleshpot a sidebar all to himself, since his sale had been bigger than any in the previous two years and perhaps this was an indication that the economy was at last "turning around." He had been bought by an agent, George Slavino, who was representing Henrietta Farms in Kentucky. Slavino had overridden the other bidders: Centennial Farms, Hickory Hill Farm, Mack Miller and D. Wayne Lucas. A Fasig-Tipton spokesman was quoted as saying that even stronger yearlings were still to come on Wednesday and Thursday nights.

I guess it's a big pleasure to see someone drop five hundred and thirty thousand on an untried horse. If you glance through the sales book, you see that a solid third of some famous sire's progeny never race and a third to half of those never win. So you are looking at substantial odds that this half-a-million-dollar purchase is never going to do any more than crop grass. That's a pretty good price for a lawn mower.

I got over to Fleshpot's stall around three forty-five. He was inside and the big fan in the doorway was making his mane do a little dance. He gave me a perfunctory look, clomped one foot down on the floor, then went back to staring at the wall.

"My man, Fleshpot," I said, "how does it feel to bring in half a million bucks?"

The colt raised and lowered his head. Maybe he felt he deserved even more. These chestnuts have almost a red in them, their fur is so glossy. Even in the dimness of his stall Fleshpot seemed to shine.

"Hey, leave the horse alone," someone said. He didn't shout but his voice was louder than was nice. It was the guy with the Three Stooges haircut who was the agent's assistant. He had a little potbelly that looked like an incipient basketball and it shook as he walked toward me. He was wearing a white short-sleeved shirt and khaki pants.

"I'm just saying hello to an old buddy," I said. "Where're Rolf and Harry?"

At that moment Harry came out of the office. He didn't seem pleased to see me but he gave me a nod.

"Hey, you must of been excited last night," I said. "How're you feeling?"

"Okay." Harry looked away from me.

"Where's your cousin?" I asked.

"He had to go to the dentist," said Harry.

"So are you guys glad to have made a big bundle? The owner must be tickled pink."

"We just want the guy who bought the horse to come and take him away," said the fellow with the haircut. "It's a big responsibility."

Harry watched me a moment without speaking, then returned to the office. I gave him a little wave but he didn't see it.

"Well, you tell the guy to watch his backside," I said.

I wandered back toward the Pavilion. It seemed if I was a guy whose feelings got easily hurt, then my feelings would have been hurt. I'd spent a chunk of time chatting with Harry and Rolf and now Harry acted like he didn't know me. But maybe he was nervous of the guy with the haircut or maybe the burden of caring for a half-million-dollar piece of dog meat had softened his brain.

However, it was too nice a day for insecure thoughts. The birds were tweedling and the pretty horses were strolling back and forth. I went up to the office on the second floor of the

Pavilion, changed into my brown uniform and got ready to protect the paintings from marauders and Philistines. Ms. Fletcher was just coming into the office as I was leaving. She was wearing a pretty yellow dress with a string of lapis around her neck.

"Hey, hey, hey," I said.

"Please be good enough to keep your remarks to yourself, Mr. Plotz," she replied.

I thought how I only had a few more days of being humble. "How about you and me having some chow together Saturday night?"

She stared at me with a look which she had probably practiced a hundred times in the mirror, a look which made her believe: With this look I can make strong men weep. She said: "Do you have any idea how quickly I can have you replaced?"

"In a nanosecond?" I asked.

"Faster." She proceeded into her office, being careful not to brush against me. Regretfully, I wondered where she had been when that black colt had been stomping on the gentry the previous evening. One of the sad things in this world is that you can never pick the people who should get stomped.

I wandered around the balcony for a while frowning at the folks who had come to admire the artwork. Now and then I patted Mr. Finney's bronze head and together we commiserated about the state of women today. Finney had a ferocious set of upper choppers so you weren't sure if he was going to grin at you or bite you. I tried to imagine a place called the Victor Plotz Pavilion but the only image I could conjure up was a plaque over a jail cell.

I kept expecting to see Paul Butterworth, then kept remembering that he had been pulled off the case, which made me realize that I didn't have to take this little job of guarding the paintings as seriously as previously. I mean, if Ms. Fletcher fired me, then I would simply go visit the Queen of Softness and we would play with the rubber duckies in her hot tub.

So shortly after six I took an unannounced fifteen-minute break and wandered off into the sales paddock. Around five-thirty the flat track had dumped out its mass of forty thousand fans and there was quite a crowd drifting around the barns. The bar was full and folks were strolling along with mint juleps in plastic glasses. You could always tell the important people because they were wearing little blue pins showing a horse's head stuck on their lapels or bosoms, which indicated that they could be let into the Pavilion, which also suggested that they had big money, although of course some were just reporters or staff people. Even Ms. Fletcher had a little blue pin.

When I got over to Barn Three West where Fleshpot was quartered, I saw that my dear butt biter was out of his stall and being checked over by a couple of strangers in expensive suits who I took to be his new owners or perhaps only their agents. Harry Macklin was holding the colt's bridle and the unfriendly guy in the Three Stooges haircut was standing back by the green wall of the barn with his arms crossed. The guys in the suits were dark-haired and healthy-looking. One was tall and lean and I recognized him as the guy who had done the bidding the previous night: Mr. George Slavino himself. I guessed he was in his mid-forties. The other guy had lifted up Fleshpot's left rear hoof and was poking at it with a little tool. Slavino was patting Fleshpot's shoulder in an absentminded way. Harry only had a hand on the bridle, no more.

I walked over a little closer. The guy holding the hoof in his paw was talking to the fellow with the haircut, saying that the truck had been delayed, but that it should be there about eight. All the paperwork had been taken care of and Fleshpot was about to go off and start a new life. I sure hoped he would be a winner. Although of course they wouldn't call him Fleshpot. They would name him Crimson Blazes or Little Lucy's Heart

Throb or something like that. All prospective names have to be submitted to the jockey club for discussion, just to make sure that two horses don't wind up with the same moniker. Some years after a horse is retired, its name can come back into circulation unless the nag happened to become famous. Sad to say there will be no more horses named Man o' War or Native Dancer. And the Jockey Club makes sure that a horse isn't given a name that is too silly or too political or too obscene. If you wanted to name your horse Prick on the Run, you'd be out of luck.

I was curious as to what Fleshpot might be called because I wanted to keep an eye peeled for him. Next spring, he would be out on the track shouldering his way among the other two-year-olds. Maybe he would even make the Kentucky Derby. So I walked over to George Slavino, who was still patting Fleshpot's shoulder, and cleared my throat in an attention-getting way.

"Excuse me," I said. "I recognize you as the gentleman who did the bidding for this proud chunk of horseflesh last night."

Slavino turned and looked at me, or maybe he just wiped his eyes across me because it wasn't really a look. He took in my brown uniform and my brown cap with the words "Henry Brown Limited" without enthusiasm. "What is your interest in the matter?" he asked.

I gave him a smile, one of my two-dollar smiles. "I've become fond of this horse," I said. "And if you hadn't bought him, perhaps I would have popped for him myself. I was curious what you're planning on naming him, just so I can keep a lookout for him next year."

"That's up to Henrietta Farms to decide," the fellow said, and he turned away.

Now this was slightly offensive, but at that moment I had something else on my mind. Slavino stood with his back to Fleshpot, maybe two feet away from the horse. Harry Macklin had his hand on the horse's neck, resting against the bridle but not really holding it. The other fellow had dropped the colt's left rear foot and was looking at me in a manner that lacked warmth. You know how the word "supercilious" originally meant above the eyebrows? He was giving me an above-the-eyebrow kind of look. The fellow with the Three Stooges haircut was taking a few unfriendly steps in my direction. Fleshpot was staring straight ahead as if not thinking about anything, not rolling in the green grass, or chomping on his feed, or those big races in his future. Like there were only zeros passing in front of his brown eyes.

So now I proceeded to startle these four guys, maybe even startle the horse. I walked about two feet in front of Fleshpot and turned my rear end in his direction. Nothing happened. I backed toward him another foot. Nothing still again. I bent over, raised my fanny and wiggled it back and forth. Nothing. I backed another foot toward Fleshpot, wagging my fanny right under his nose and saying, "Horsey, horsey, horsey!" Nothing again.

"What in the world's going on here?" asked Slavino.

"This isn't Fleshpot," I said.

"Who?" asked the man in a tone that combined indignation and outrage.

"This isn't Hip Fifty-seven. He's a ringer."

"What the hell you talking about?" said the fellow with the haircut. He gave me a push to get me out of the way and I stumbled back.

"Don't touch the sacred flesh," I said.

"Who is this guy?" asked the other man.

"He guards the paintings in the Pavilion," said Harry.

"I'm a pal of Fleshpot's," I said, "and this isn't Fleshpot. I mean, did he try to bite my ass?"

"Who is Fleshpot?" asked Slavino. I must say that three of these guys seemed a trifle enraged while Harry didn't look like he was feeling much of anything. As for the ringer, or what I thought was a ringer, he just kept staring off at the blue sky.

"Fleshpot was the name I gave to the horse that used to live in this stall, otherwise known as Hip Fifty-seven, before this similar-looking horse was swapped for him."

The guy with the haircut took the bridle away from Harry. "Go get security," he told him.

"You must be clean out of your mind," said Slavino, pushing his hand through his slicked-back brown hair to make sure the top of his cranium was still in place. The fellow who had been holding the ringer's rear hoof slowly shook his head as if I were one more example that the human gene pool was turning into so much caked mud.

Well, considering these guys' reaction, I thought I might be wrong. Maybe being sold for half a million smackers had affected Fleshpot's wits and he thought my ass was no longer good enough to bite. If I got sold for big bucks, I'm sure I'd get a swollen head as well. Also, as I looked along the line of stalls, I saw Harry trotting back with two Pinkertons jogging beside him. I thought of Ms. Fletcher and her paintings. I thought of Lawyer Arnold Steinfeld and his possible subpoenas. I thought of Mrs. Florence Ross who was not the daughter of Betsy Ross.

"Okay, okay," I said. "I must of made a mistake." And I tiptoed away.

Just before I reentered the Pavilion one of the Pinkertons caught up with me. "I don't know what you were pulling back there," he said, "but if you don't stay out of the sales paddock, we'll file a complaint."

"You think a horse could be stolen from here?" I asked, perfectly seriously.

The Pinkerton wrinkled his face into a definition of the word "contemptuous." He was a healthy hunk of hamburger, well over six feet, with officer's medals on his lapels. "It'd be easier to get money out of Fort Knox," he said. "We've got thirty men here. We'd catch whoever tried."

"You didn't catch Jesse James," I said.

He let that remark drift past him as if it were a big fat fly that was not worth his attention and turned on his heel. I went back upstairs to the paintings. Ms. Fletcher was waiting for me at the top.

"And where have you been, Mr. Plotz?"

"I had to take a dump," I told her.

She too turned on her heel. Like I was the opposite of a captain leading a cavalry charge. I was making people run in the other direction.

By now the Pavilion was beginning to fill up for Wednesday night's auction. Lots of folks were ogling the paintings of pricey horses cropping dandelions or scenes of stately manor houses of years gone by. I walked slowly around the perimeter, not even patting old Finney's head as I passed. My mind, as they say, was in a buzz. Let me admit right off that I have been wrong about things before. Do not think that Vic Plotz cannot confess to making a mistake. And really I had no proof about Fleshpot except my own intuition. Maybe they had given Fleshpot some mood-changing drugs. Maybe he was depressed at leaving his life of leisure behind. I mean, if a horse looks like Fleshpot, smells like Fleshpot and tastes like Fleshpot, then isn't he Fleshpot? That was the great question which I set myself.

A few minutes past eight o'clock the auction cranked up and the first horse, Hip Sixty-three, a bay colt, was led into the auction ring and immediately relieved himself. The announcer chatted the horse up in his dulcet British tones and the auctioneer tried to start the bidding at fifty grand but had to drop back down to thirty before anyone would nibble. I strolled around the big circle with my hands behind my back. Half my attention was here in the Pavilion and half was over in Barn Three West where Fleshpot or the horse that looked like Fleshpot was about to be trucked off to his new owner's. But if he wasn't Fleshpot, then wouldn't the switch be discovered soon enough? Surely before the horse raced there would be another blood test and then the caca would hit the air conditioner. But how many weeks or months would pass before that happened? The auctioneer said, "Going once, going twice," then smacked down the gavel. The first horse of the night was sold for ninety grand and the second horse was brought in.

Around nine I decided to take my lunch break and wander over to Fleshpot's stall. I made my way down the stairs and into the paddock area. It was a warm night. The wealthy ladies were wearing their loose summer dresses. Almost immediately I felt a hand gripping my arm. And not too lightly, I might add. It was the oversized Pinkerton who had chatted with me earlier.

"Didn't I tell you to stay out of this area?"

"It's my lunch break. I haven't eaten all day."

The Pinkerton called over one of his younger flunkies, a pink-cheeked kid who looked about eighteen. "Show this fellow where the snack bar is and stay with him while he eats. Then make sure he goes back upstairs."

So me and the kid walked over to the lunch counter and I ordered a couple of burgers. As I waited for the burgers to get cooked I asked the kid if he liked the Red Sox. He didn't answer. I asked if he liked the Yankees and he still didn't answer. Like he was too proud to speak to an employee of Henry Brown Limited.

"You ever fucked a chicken?" I inquired.

No answer.

"You got to hold them just right or they'll burst out of your hands. A big fat hen is the best. Mmmm, I get excited just thinking about it."

"You're perverted," said the kid.

I gave him a big smile and paid for my burgers. At least I had gotten him to speak.

For the rest of the evening, I strolled around the second floor of the Pavilion. The auction continued. A bay colt was sold to D. Wayne Lucas for two hundred grand. Mrs. C. V. Whitney bought a gray filly for two-fifty. Another colt went to some Japanese buyer for three-fifty. But nothing touched Fleshpot's sale of the night before. Rich folks were chatting on portable phones and through the big windows I could see the hoi polloi eyeballing the crowd inside hoping to pick out a celebrity. A few more red "sold" stickers went up on a few more of Henry Brown's paintings. In the meantime, the horses came and went, each spending its four or five minutes in the auction ring, and two-thirds of them took their nervous little dump, which the black guy with the broom and dustpan deftly swept out of the green plastic sawdust.

The last horse, Hip One Twenty-six, was auctioned off around eleven-thirty and folks began to leave. I had to stay until twelve and then Ms. Fletcher said she wanted to have a few words with me.

"There have been complaints made about you, Mr. Plotz." We were in her small office and she was on the other side of the desk. Like she wanted to keep a large object between us.

"Do tell," I said.

"Tomorrow when you arrive you are to stay out of the sales paddock and I expect you to be here at four p.m. on the dot."

"What do these complaining people say that I have done?" I asked.

Ms. Fletcher made one of those above-the-eyebrows expressions which I was growing used to. "They speak of your being a nuisance. Believe me, if I could replace you for tomorrow, I surely would."

Although I was tempted to tell her to piss up a rope, I kept a civil tongue in my mouth. "Oh, Ms. Fletcher, I'm sorry to have caused you any embarrassment."

That was how it went for the next few minutes. By the time I left the Pavilion most everybody else had left and there were only a few doleful sweepers getting the place neat and tidy for the coming day. Now and then I could hear the whinny of a horse. Something big stamping in a stall. A nighthawk squawked and I heard the buzz of its wings as it dove past the lights to catch a bug. I went to retrieve my Raleigh. To tell the truth I am mostly a chipper sort of guy but all this talk today about Bad, Bad Victor Plotz was beginning to wear me down. Like even the bubonic plague has the rats to chummy up to.

I unlocked my bike chain and pedaled back down the sandy paths to the front of the Pavilion, since all the other gates were locked by this time. I turned left on East Avenue. Across the street on the other side of the fence, where the Oklahoma Track was located, there was extra parking for the yearling sales. Through the bushes I could see a couple of cars. Then I squeezed my handbrakes tight and came to a squeaky halt. Yanking the handlebars to the right, I made a U-turn across the street toward the parking lot. The gate was still open. There, parked all by itself, was a green Volkswagen Beetle with a raccoon tail attached to the radio antenna: Paul Butterworth's car. Had he been here? If so, why hadn't I seen him? And if he hadn't been at the yearling sales, then why was his car in the lot?

7

Normally I sleep like a baby, but that Wednesday night, or Thursday morning, I had a rough and rocky ride full of unanswered questions. Had the horse that refused to bite my backside indeed been Fleshpot? Had Butterworth's car simply broken down and that was why it was still in the lot? Had Butterworth been hiding out at the sales paddock, trying a little sneakiness so he could catch me doing something I shouldn't? All night long I flipped back and forth like a trout on a grill.

Around seven-thirty I dragged my puttylike *cuerpo* from bed, showered, shaved the overly familiar kisser, made coffee, gave the cat, Moshe III, a couple of slices of turkey, looked up Butterworth's number in the phone book and gave him a call. I mean, if I couldn't sleep why should he?

One of the things that irritate me most in this life are people who have answering machines with an agenda. I know a guy who sings, so you have to listen to a lousy rendition of "Ghost Riders in the Sky" before you can leave your message. Another guy tells jokes. "Say, folks, Bob's joke for the day is: Why did the chicken cross the road? Hunh? Just to show the armadillo that it could be done." Then he laughs.

Paul Butterworth's answering machine read a little poem.

Likes

He likes to walk in the forest alone, go days
Without seeing another person and not care
Where the deer path takes him. He's given up
Maps in favor of wandering. He likes the word
Aimless and the birdsongs he knows are important.
He likes bramble and thicket, stand and riprap.
He likes to watch the fat robin at work in the morning
And the gray owl rise through the tree in the starlight.

It went on like that for a couple of minutes and I held the phone to my ear, not because the poem spoke to my tormented soul but because sometimes an answering machine doesn't mean that the person isn't at home. Sometimes the person is hiding *behind* his answering machine and he is just waiting for you to identify yourself before he picks up the phone. I can't tell you how much I disapprove of this.

So I listened to the whole poem, then I listened to Butterworth give his number and say he's sorry but he can't come to the phone right now, then there was a beep and I said, "Butterworth, are you back there? This is Vic Plotz. Butterworth, pick up the phone." And I chattered on like that through the end of the tape.

But I was still not satisfied. I mean, these kids were heavy sleepers and maybe Butterworth was asleep. So I got dressed, retrieved my Yugo from the back lot and drove over to Butterworth's place, which the phone book had told me was on

Franklin Square, an area of big old mansions most of which have been broken up into apartments or condos. By the time I left the Algonquin it was eight o'clock and Saratoga was just waking up, old guys were toddling off to buy their *Racing Forms* and the sun was bright in the sky.

Maybe I spent five minutes knocking on Butterworth's door on the third floor of a Victorian monstrosity on Clinton Street. Sometimes it seems you can tell that nobody is at home just by the way the knocking reverberates inside. Like if there was a person in there, the knocking wouldn't sound so hollow.

After a while, I went back down to the lobby where there was a row of mailboxes. I located Butterworth's mailbox, then felt a little chill when I saw that his mail hadn't been picked up from the previous day.

So after that I drove out to the Humphrey S. Finney Pavilion to see if Butterworth's Volkswagen Beetle was still in the lot across the street. It was. I got out of the Yugo and walked around the VW as if I expected the little car to tell me something. The doors weren't even locked, for crying out loud. The VW was as empty as an empty Coke bottle.

I stood in the parking lot considering the possibilities and not liking any of them. My watch said it was eight-twenty. I decided to drive out to the lake and talk to Charlie Bradshaw.

When Charlie was a copper, he lived in town just like anybody else. He had a wife. He had respectable cousins in the community. And he was a sergeant, a guy with a little clout. However, as he once told me, it also seemed that all these folks, and others as well, owned a piece of him, so that he was left with less and less of himself. Like he was a fragment in his own life. So he quit the police force, left his wife, said goodbye to his cousins and got this place on Lake Saratoga that is small but occupies about three lots and has some room around it. The response in town, of course, was that everybody thought he was off his rocker, but Charlie didn't care about that anymore. He developed a little smile. His ulcer went away. Then, after a year, I came up from New York City to keep him company.

That Thursday morning I found him out on his dock reading a book. "Do you know," Charlie told me straight off, "that Jesse James might have sung at his own funeral?"

"How odd," I said.

"It seems this stranger showed up who nobody knew and completely took charge. He was one of the pallbearers and he even sang."

"What did he sing?"

"It doesn't say."

"I bet it wasn't 'Be-Bop-A-Lula.' "

Charlie didn't bother to answer. "But this writer argues that the stranger was Jesse in disguise and the corpse in the coffin was a ringer."

"Speaking of ringers," I said, "I got a serious problem."

Charlie checked my face for whimsy, mockery and/or sarcasm. Seeing it was clean, he asked, "What seems to be the matter?"

He got me a cup of coffee and dragged up another rusty lawn chair and we sat down on the dock. Some old guys were fishing out on the water. It was still too early for the motorboats and the jerks who like to make a lot of noise. The sun was hot and I took off my gray jacket.

"Have I told you about Fleshpot?" I asked.

"Didn't you say he was a horse?"

So I described my innocent folderol of passing myself off as a prospective buyer and how I had these grooms and agents jumping their expensive horseflesh through hoops for my idle frolic. Then I got to Fleshpot and discussed his strange attraction for the human backside and how he had been auctioned off for half a million, more than any other horse during two days of the sales. Then I described how I had seen him yesterday and why I thought the horse I had seen wasn't Fleshpot. Like my buns to him were so much broken glass. Then I talked about Butterworth, who Charlie already knew, and how I hadn't seen him since night before last, how his Beetle was still in the parking lot and his mail hadn't been picked up.

"But there are Pinkertons all over the place, plus hundreds of other people," said Charlie. "How could the horse have been stolen?" He wasn't necessarily doubting me, he just wondered how it could be done.

I pulled up my slacks a little bit so my ankles could get the sun. "Well, I've been thinking how I haven't seen Butterworth since the horse got loose in the crowd late Tuesday night." I described the black colt galloping all over the sales paddock and whanging into people, which Charlie had already read about in the *Saratogian*. I described how I had dragged a woman to safety out from under the plummeting hooves of this maddened brute and how the black colt had finally been subdued.

"What I been thinking," I said, "is if Fleshpot was swapped for a ringer, the best time to do it was when he was being walked back to his stall after the auction and when this black horse was tearing all over the place getting people hysterical. Harry Macklin was walking Fleshpot back. What if his cousin Rolf was in a stall with the ringer and when everyone was looking the other way, they do a swap? That blaze on the horse's forehead has got to be dye. And they could have marked up poor Fleshpot to look like anything, Groucho Marx even, then got him out the next morning pretending he was a stable pony."

"What's happened to the other horse now?" asked Charlie.

"He was supposed to have been shipped out last night." I explained how my innocent activities had made me persona non grata in the sales paddock so I didn't know for sure if the horse had been shipped out or not.

"You make friends wherever you go, don't you," said Charlie.

"I'm a lovable guy," I said. "So what are we going to do about this problem?"

Now I got to say, many times in the past Charlie has come to me and made a similar statement: "What are we going to do, Victor?" And I have said, "We? Why we, white boy?" or words to that effect. I'm the kind of guy who mostly has to have his arm twisted. But Charlie is not like that. Even though he likely had other plans, he didn't drag his feet. You see how it works? I teach him meanness; he teaches me softness.

"I'll go into town and start making inquiries. I'll have to talk to the Fasig-Tipton people and the Pinkertons. Probably even the police. What do you think happened to Butterworth?"

"I don't like to think. You see, I was following Fleshpot back to the stall after the sale. Like I wanted to shake his big right hoof and tell him he was a champion. Butterworth was tailing along behind me. Then this black colt gets loose and everybody starts shouting and I get distracted. But what if Butterworth didn't get distracted? What if he kept following Fleshpot and saw the swap? I mean, we're talking about a half-a-million-dollar piece of property."

Around ten o'clock I left Charlie's and drove over to Rosemary's lunch counter for a late breakfast. She gets a lot of farmers and truck drivers so her clientele is about ninety-nine percent male. Often Rosemary has a local girl working the counter and some old guy in the back doing the eggs as Rosemary sits behind the cash register on a high stool as if on a throne. In a glass case under the register, she plies her objects of art: sequined caps and blouses and neckties and halters and bikini bottoms. These truck drivers and farmers are often hefty guys and none of them will see forty again. One imagines hefty wives in the background. Rosemary does a good business with her sequined bikini bottoms, jockstraps, halter tops, neckties and beanies. So you have to think of that when you are driving through this part of the country late in the evening and you're passing houses with their shades drawn and you think the old folks are inside playing checkers or watching the tube. But most likely it is some fat old guy and his fat old wife dressed up in Rosemary's sequined underwear doing the hip-hop or the dirty boogie. My, those sequins sparkle when you dance.

The Queen of Softness gave me a peck on the cheek and I sat down on a stool by the cash register. She won't let me eat eggs in her place anymore, although she pushes them on the other folks. It's sad: when we were young, we snuck around doing reefers and Jack Daniel's. Now that we're old, we sneak eggs and bacon. At Rosemary's I get the bran muffin, the oatmeal and sometimes the whole-grain pancakes.

I told her what had been going on at the yearling sales: the black colt galloping around, the popularity of yours truly, Butterworth's disappearance. She had gotten friendly with Butterworth when he was following us around at the track. They even had a few close chats about art: poetry and sequins. When I said that he seemed to be missing, she grew a little anxious.

"But you have to find him, Vic."

Rosemary has a low voice which I like to think of as sultry. She was wearing loose-fitting shorts and a blouse made out of some silky material with a tiger-skin pattern. Her hair is platinum blond with gray roots. One used to say, "If you have it, flaunt it." But flaunting is too subtle for Rosemary, she likes to fling it around.

"Maybe he's just shacking up with someone," I suggested.

"That might be true but you still have to find out. He's just a kid."

"Charlie's checking on it."

"And what are you doing, just filling your face?"

I explained about being persona non grata, but that wasn't good enough either. "You can use the phone, can't you?"

The upshot of it was that thirty minutes later I was back in Rosemary's bungalow making various calls. Rosemary's place is more like a lair. It's the animal paintings on black velvet which create that impression and also the upholstery: fake leopard and zebra, giraffe and tiger. There is also a big bearskin rug made out of some plastic material. Rosemary doesn't believe in killing animals for their fur. Although her place is absolutely jam-packed with animal skins, it is all ersatz.

I called up the Fasig-Tipton offices and got the name and number of the place that had bought Fleshpot: Henrietta Farms in Oxbridge, Kentucky. Then I got the name and phone number of the agent who had sold the horse: Henry O'Leary. He was the agent for ten different horses in the sales paddock. They gave me his telephone number over in the barn. I called and identified myself as a reporter for the *Standard*.

"So how does it feel to sell a horse for five hundred and thirty thousand dollars?" I asked.

"I'm only pleased that I can meet the expectations of the people who have entrusted me with their fine thoroughbreds."

That was how O'Leary talked, and I was glad that I wasn't a real reporter otherwise I would have climbed the walls.

O'Leary told me that Hip Fifty-seven (it was hard for me not to call him Fleshpot) had been owned by Sycamore Farms, which had sent two horses up to the sales from Livermore, Kentucky. The other horse, Hip Seventy, had been sold the previous evening for one hundred and twenty thousand. It seemed odd to me that both the buyer and seller might be in Kentucky and yet the horse would be sent nearly a thousand miles in order to be sold. O'Leary also explained that he had four assistants working for him in the sales paddock and a dozen grooms. A few he had brought from Kentucky and others he had hired locally.

I asked him about the grooms who were taking care of Flesh-pot and he gave me their names. Harry and Rolf Macklin, which of course I knew. He said they had been hired locally by one of his assistants, Jerry Pennyfeather, several weeks before the sales. I wanted to ask if Pennyfeather had a haircut like Moe in the Three Stooges, but such a question seemed to push my repor-torial expertise. I asked if Hip Fifty-seven was still on the prem-ises but O'Leary said no, he had been picked up the previous evening. He didn't know if the horse had been shipped back to Kentucky or was still up in Saratoga.

"Do you think the buyer was happy with Hip Fifty-seven?" I asked.

"I'd think so but I doubt that the buyer even saw the horse. The whole deal was done through an agent, George Slavino."

"Does he work out of Kentucky as well?"

"No, he's down in Newburgh and he's got a couple of horses running at Belmont and Aqueduct."

By the time I left Rosemary's animal pad in the midafternoon I had a list of names and phone numbers which was clear evi-dence of time spent on the telephone and which Rosemary took as proof of hard work. Unfortunately, I wasn't sure what to do with it.

I drove over to the sales paddock and parked in the Fasig-Tipton lot next to Butterworth's VW. This was the last day of the sales and there were fewer people about. It was about three-thirty and I had to start work in half an hour. From the flat track I could hear the bugle calling for what was probably the sixth race. It was a windy afternoon and dust devils were spinning across the dirt of the parking lot. It looked like it would rain by evening.

I crossed the street to the sales paddock. Instead of entering by the Pavilion, I walked up to Madison so I could enter through the side gate and wouldn't have to stroll by the Pinkerton office.

You know that walk you use when you expect someone is going to shout: "Hey, you, stop!" Like it feels you have a cramp between your shoulder blades.

I slipped through the side entrance and skirted the fence until I got to Barn Three West. Four of O'Leary's stalls were shut up and three more had had the signs taken down, indicating that the horses had been sold but not yet taken away. A groom I didn't recognize was walking a bay colt back and forth for the pleasure of a guy in a three-piece khaki suit. I walked up to the groom.

"Have you seen Harry or Rolf Macklin?"

The guy looked at me with sleepy boredom. He was blond and probably in his late twenties. "I haven't seen them today. Check the office." He motioned with his head toward a door between two of the shut-up stalls.

I went over and knocked. I couldn't see through the screen but when a voice answered, I opened up. The guy with the Stooge haircut was sitting behind a beat-up desk looking through some papers. He glanced up at me from under his bangs.

"Mr. Pennyfeather?" I asked.

"What d'you want?"

"Is Harry or Rolf Macklin around?"

"Didn't security tell you to stay away from here?" Pennyfeather sounded tired rather than angry.

I had been hoping that he wouldn't recognize me, but when you're as handsome as I am, then it is hard to be anonymous. Maybe it was my shining dynamic eyes or my imposing masculine figure. Maybe it was my distinguished Jewish Afro or my nose which sets off my face like the figurehead of the Lady of the Deep might set off a schooner. In any case, he knew who he was talking to.

"I just wanted a few words with Harry or Rolf."

Pennyfeather picked up the phone, dialed a number and said, "He's back." Then he hung up.

"You don't learn, do you?" he said.

"For crying out loud, can't you tell me if they're here or not?"

Pennyfeather returned to his papers. I was tempted to pee on his floor, but instead I went back outside, hoping to find another groom to talk to. But I hadn't been outside for a single minute when two Pinkertons in uniform came jogging around the corner of the barn. When they saw me they got happy looks like piggy people sitting down to a bucket of ice cream.

I stuck out my hands in front of me, palms outward. "Don't touch the flesh," I said.

They didn't quite touch the flesh but they grabbed the clothing which enclosed it with a certain roughness. Then they proceeded to walk me back toward the Pavilion.

"Are you guys gay lovers by any chance?" I asked.

They walked me a little faster. "You're a nasty piece of goods," said the guy on my left.

"Hey, I got friends who hold me in deep regard."

"Perverts," said the guy on my right.

But then something nice happened. Just as they were hustling me past the Fasig-Tipton offices, a woman came out, took a gander at me and burst into a big smile. "There you are," she said happily.

The Pinkertons let go of me so fast that I nearly fell. Then I smoothed out the wrinkles on my gray sport coat as I looked back at the woman and gave her a peek at my cheerful choppers. She was middle-aged and wearing an expensive summer dress with patterns of flowers and her brown hair was piled up on her head in a way that suggested hours in a beauty shop. I didn't think I knew her but as she continued to smile, I realized she was the woman I had dragged away from the hysterical black colt on Tuesday night.

"I didn't get a chance to thank you," said the woman. "You probably saved my life."

"Shucks," I said. "Anyone would have done it."

I didn't know who the lady was but the Pinkertons knew her and she was wearing one of these little blue pins which let the rich folks in and out of the Pavilion.

"Well, I just wanted to say that I was grateful," said the woman. She gave me another big smile and walked away.

I winked at my Pinkertons. "Are you telling me that fine lady is perverted?" I asked.

One of them hissed at me: "Go into the Pavilion and don't leave. And after tomorrow, don't come back."

I wanted to say that I was supposed to work for another week, but when I got upstairs Ms. Fletcher quickly disabused me of that idea.

"I have someone to replace you for the last week," she said.

She said this in the same tone of voice that she might have said, "I just won the lottery."

I carped about this for a while, not because I wanted to stay but because I wanted to gouge some extra money out of her. At last she agreed to cut a check that included an extra day's pay. I went to put on my snazzy brown uniform.

I had expected a quiet night at the Pavilion, strolling around, saying goodbye to the paintings, patting Humphrey S. Finney's bronze head for one last time, watching the last sixty-five horses get auctioned. Instead, a dramatic event occurred. I wish I could say that it was something I merely witnessed, but as it turned out I was at its very center.

The excitement occurred around eight-thirty and only a few yearlings had been sold. A bay filly in the auction ring was whinnying ferociously. The spotters were shouting "Hep!" and "Yo!" and the bidding had already reached two hundred grand. All of a sudden about ten uniformed cops entered the Pavilion, led by a couple of plainclothesmen. The auctioneer paused as the cops hurried up the stairs to the second floor. There they split up, half going one way, half going the other. I figured that someone had given Fasig-Tipton a rubber check or perhaps news had come that one of these rich folks had scragged his mother-in-law. I was standing by Mr. Finney's bronze bust buffing my nails. As the coppers got closer to me, I got less and less happy. Like they were staring at me in the way ten thousand piranhas might stare at a Guernsey cow that has just stumbled into their pond. Down amongst the red seats, such a large number of well-dressed necks were cranking around to see the copper action that the creaking of their spines was like the passionate clicking of castanets. The auctioneer slowed his chatter. When the two points of the pincer action of Saratoga's finest were within ten feet of me, I stepped away from the bust of Humphrey S. Finney because I didn't want to incriminate him. Several people took snapshots of my embarrassment.

The lead plainclothesmen stopped in front of me. "Victor Plotz, I'm arresting you on suspicion of the murder of Paul Butterworth."

Then the handcuffs were slapped across my wrists and I was led away. I could see in the coppers' eyes and in the eyes of some other folks a touch of regret that I hadn't tried to resist arrest so I could have been pummeled into the carpet as well as handcuffed. When we reached the stairs, Ms. Fletcher came out of her office. The smile she gave me was the first I had seen on her handsome face.

8

You would have had to have known Chief Harvey L. Peterson, Commissioner of Public Safety, in his prime to realize what an imposing figure he could be. Tall, muscular, well-fed, he was like a prize bull in a three-piece blue suit. Now he was a few months short of retirement and sick. Too much chemo, too many morbid thoughts. Like the grim reaper had his number. These days he wore a gray wig and his blue suit draped his body like a scarecrow's duds. But even though his voice was no longer the bullhorn that it used to be, it hadn't lost any of its meanness.

"If it turns out you don't have an alibi," he told me with a smile, "you'll go back to the slammer and I'll personally make sure they don't set bail."

Let me say that a night in jail can drive all the witty remarks right out of a man. It's the big deflation. My back hurt and I had some itchy places where something had bitten me in the wee hours of the morning. I tried to summon up the strength to tell Peterson to piss up a rope, but instead I just sat there in the visitor's chair and fiddled with my hands. It was nine-thirty Friday morning and I was in Peterson's fancy office in police headquarters. In the old days it had been decorated with pictures of prize Irish setters which had made Peterson's name a piece of magic in the world of doggy show biz. But now he had stopped showing Irish setters due to his ill health and instead the office was decorated with pictures of Peterson shaking hands with famous people. Like he gets his kicks from pressing his gray palm against the palms of celebrities: a range of folks from the ex-veep Dan Quayle and the ex-con Ollie North, to Mrs. C. V. Whitney and the ballet guy Peter Martins. I imagined all these people slipping their famous paws against Peterson's hand, feeling the grayness there, the inclemency of soul, then rushing off to scrub the cop from their fingers.

But it was more than a night in jail that had upset me. Paul Butterworth was dead. His body had been snagged by a fisherman in Lake Saratoga the previous day. In his wallet was a card from the lawyer, Arnold Steinfeld, and Steinfeld told the cops that Butterworth had been tailing me. The possibly criminal rapport between me and the stock market had been discussed. Other people had been questioned, and to make a long story short, the last time that Butterworth had been seen alive was Tuesday night at the yearling sales. The present argument was that I had scragged him when the black colt had been galloping all over the paddock and people had been distracted by the commotion.

"And why did I kill him?" I had asked the lieutenant in charge the previous evening, a no-neck monster named Ron Novack, who has turned himself into a physical freak with his weight-lifting regimen. Like the body he was born with wasn't good enough for him and he wanted to become a *Tyrannosaurus rex*.

"Because he had figured out your stock scam," Novack had told me, "and he was going to tell Steinfeld."

The difficulty with living in a small town is that you know a lot of people for a long time. Over the years I had made various humorous but perfectly harmless remarks about Novack's physique which he had taken personally. I mean, even though he truly was a no-neck monster, he objected to being called a no-neck monster. Wasn't that his own hang-up? If he didn't want to be called a no-neck monster, then why did he pump iron twenty hours a day? It made no sense to me.

In any case, Novack saw in this occasion a chance to pay me back for the slights I had tossed upon his honor. He was an ex-military guy and honor was important to him. Besides, since he didn't like me, Novack assumed I must be a lawbreaker and now, he felt, he had the case to prove it.

The previous night when I'd been snatched from the Humphrey S. Finney Pavilion, Novack had taken me directly to the morgue at the hospital. Of course, he didn't say where he was taking me. I was handcuffed and a couple of big guys were holding on to my arms. We drove to the hospital and I got pushed and shoved down to the basement to a room that I first thought was a kind of kitchen but there were no stoves, just lots of stainless-steel cabinets. Then a small door was pulled open and a stretcher comes sliding out with a body lying on it. Novack pulled back the sheet and I saw that the body was Paul Butterworth and he was as naked as a jaybird and they had already done an autopsy and stitched his front back up with thick black thread in a way that I can tell will never heal.

Now I liked Butterworth, moderately, and I am truly knocked for a loop that he is lying there on that cold stretcher and he doesn't look good: all bloated from the water and something has eaten his eyes and he has got this lousy black stitching running up the middle of him and his silly flattop haircut will never stand up straight again. Novack is looking at me in a smug sort of way and the other two coppers are looking at me as well. Like all three of them are hoping that I will puke and confess to scragging poor Butterworth. But all I can see is that he is dead and that it is sad that he's dead and even if I had hated him, I would have preferred him among the living. Nothing looks deader than a dead person, that is one of life's unfortunate truths, and I would have liked a few minutes alone with him so I could say goodbye and make my peace with him, but here were these coppers staring at me, looking to see how I would react.

The more I became aware of Novack staring at me, the angrier I got at him for wanting to shock me. Like it was a mean trick. So even though I am handcuffed, I turn to him and kick him in the leg with one of my heavy black private cop shoes, because of course I am still wearing that silly brown uniform, although I've lost the cap.

"You sadistic bastard," I told him. And for about three seconds I have the pleasure of seeing Novack hop up and down on one leg before the other two coppers "subdue" me. Isn't that a nice word? Subdue. Wham, wham, wham. If I could show you the bruises from my subduction, I gladly would.

And so not only am I charged with first degree murder, I am also charged with attempting to escape, resisting arrest and attacking a police officer with a dangerous weapon: ie, my shoe. So I had various things to think about during the still watches of the night when I was unable to sleep because the mattress was too thin and something was biting me and my kidneys hurt because those bozos in blue had whacked me there.

When I was given the chance to make a phone call around two a.m., I called Charlie. He wasn't out at the lake, but I got him at Janey Burris's, where I hoped he was snoozing or reading a book instead of being transmogrified in an act of sexual passion.

"I'll get you out as soon as I can," Charlie told me. "How was he killed?"

"Someone hit him on the head and his body was tossed in the

lake. It was just by chance he was found so quickly."

"Poor guy," said Charlie.

"Poor guy," I agreed.

So the next morning I am dragged up to Peterson's office the moment he gets in. It would be wrong to say that small-town coppers enjoy murders, but murders are for them a public occasion. I mean, they work hard all year long at boring things that will never make the newspapers, but if they turn up a corpse, then every newshound within two hundred miles wants to get a quote and a picture. It's the time when cops get to act out their fantasies about what cops should be: authoritative, heroic, deep-thinking and philosophical about the general wickedness of human behavior. Basically, for the coppers, I was a stage prop. I was the occasion for them to show off their expertise and be coplike. The number one problem was that I wasn't guilty. The number two problem was that I wouldn't keep my mouth shut.

"Sure, you can bring in the reporters," I told Peterson, "and I'll tell them how your bozos beat me up even though I was handcuffed."

"You were resisting arrest," said Peterson, shading his eyes so he wouldn't have to look at me.

"That's right, they got themselves an old fart with sixty years on his back and they handcuff him, then they pound on his kidneys because he doesn't stay as quiet as they'd like. You heard about the Rodney King case? Wait till you hear about the Vic Plotz case."

I felt sorry for Peterson. He sat at his desk supporting himself with his elbows with his left hand against his forehead. His gray wig was a trifle askew. His neck was loose in the collar of his white shirt the way a toothpick would be loose in an exhaust pipe. He simply didn't have the strength anymore to keep up his side of the chitchat. We had bandied words for nearly twenty years and now because of sickness and age, he was letting his side slip.

"Tell me again about this woman," he said, still without looking at me.

"I saved her life. At great risk to myself I dove between the hooves of an hysterical horse and dragged her away."

"And what's her name?" Peterson took the pen from his fancy desk set and raised it in anticipation.

"I don't know but she's a rich lady and the Pinkertons recognized her. All you have to do is call over there."

Several people had seen me leaving the sales paddock on my bicycle on Tuesday evening, so the only questionable period was during the time that the horse had been loose. Also, no matter how much Peterson might have wanted me to be guilty, he knew that I wasn't. I might break the law in small ways, but I wasn't about to kill someone. That was just wishful thinking on Novack's part. And there was also the problem of removing the body. I mean, could I have carried Butterworth out to the lake on the handlebars of my bike? So, even though Peterson would have liked to keep me in jail for a hundred years, he knew that was impossible and this was why he looked depressed.

"Had you been quarreling with Butterworth?" asked Peterson.

"Nah, we'd become chums. We'd gone to the track together over the weekend. Ask the Queen of Softness."

"Who?"

"My main squeeze."

We went on like that for a while, trading remarks. You know how it is when you see a person you have known for a long time? Not only are you looking at them at the particular moment, but you also get images of how they used to look and you have little flashes of how they acted on other occasions. Seeing Peterson at half his weight and two months short of retirement, I didn't actually feel sorry for him, but it was sobering. Here was a guy who had shouted at me a thousand times and now he could hardly speak above a growl. And his hands shook and you could tell he wanted to be home in bed and he wasn't about to bounce me off the walls like he had threatened to do in the past.

"I'll bet quarters to kumquats," I said, "that Butterworth was killed because he knew about Fleshpot's being stolen."

"Who?" asked Peterson again.

So I told him about the horse I called Fleshpot and how he was actually known as Hip Fifty-seven, but I could see that my explanations, instead of making things better, only made them worse. They lacked the bright light of clarity. Peterson looked at me and sighed. His face had gotten so thin that his eyes seemed twice as big.

"Lieutenant Novack talked to those Pinkertons," he said. "They had a story about some sexual thing between you and a horse. You kept trying to stick your ass in its nose."

So I told him about Fleshpot's odd habit and how this other horse had taken no interest in my backside, or anyone else's for that matter, and again Peterson sighed and looked depressed. You know how someone wants to ask you questions but what they want even more is to get you out of their sight? Peterson was torn like that. But even though he was tired and sick and wanted me to disappear, he still had a flicker of cop in him.

"So you're saying that Butterworth was killed by whoever was swapping the horses?"

"You betcha."

"But there's no evidence that the horses were swapped." Peterson said this in a voice no louder than a whisper.

"No, but there will be. In the meantime, I would look for those Macklin cousins. And I'd also talk to this Pennyfeather guy who works for the agent."

Peterson managed to scrape together a little of the indignation which had sustained him in past years. "Look, Plotz, right now you're the guy being charged with this murder, and if there're any other wrinkles in this case, we'll figure them out in our own sweet time. As for you, you're going back to a jail cell and who knows when you'll get out."

Peterson had some pleasure saying that. He gave a little smile and, briefly, he looked a little healthier. All told his pleasure lasted about fifteen seconds, because then the door opened. My back was to it and at first I only saw Peterson's expression change as the old exhaustion came back and Saratoga Springs' top copper seemed to age about twenty more years even as I watched.

I turned around to see what had broken his heart. It was a double whammy. Coming through the doorway was my buddy Charlie Bradshaw and Madame X, the lady I had dragged out from under the horse's hooves.

When the lady saw me, she gave a big smile. "There you are," she said. She was wearing a pinkish-lavenderish hat about three feet across and a dress of some gauzy material to match. Even her shoes were covered with the same pinkish lavender.

Introductions were made. The lady was Jennifer Holcomb-Smith, co-owner of Felicity Farms near Lynchburg, Virginia. The name meant nothing to me but Charlie said later that she came to the auctions every August and this year she had dropped four hundred grand on three yearlings. I could see, however, that Peterson recognized her, not that he seemed pleased to have her in his office.

"I don't know what you're accusing this man of," said Mrs. Holcomb-Smith, "but my lawyer will be here within ten minutes and I personally will guarantee bail."

Peterson put his left hand back to his forehead. "Anything else?" he asked.

"Yes," said Charlie, standing by my chair. "Even though we don't as yet have the results of the blood test, the blaze on the forehead of the horse that Victor calls Fleshpot seems to have been made with dye. And there's more dye on the left front white stocking. Evidently the two horses were exchanged just as Victor said they were."

I leaned back in the visitor's chair and basked a little. Peterson looked down at his desk. No telling what he saw there, but I bet it was nothing nice.

9

"What impresses me most," Charlie told me as we drove out to the sales paddock later that morning, "is how you managed to save the life of one of the richest women at the sales. Did you pass up a lot of poor ones first?"

"Nope, she was just the first one I saw. I guess I have a natural talent."

"A nose for money," said Charlie. "Me, I probably would have saved somebody without a dime, a panhandler or some poor homeless guy who had just wandered through the gate."

We were in Charlie's Mazda 323, which was making its usual whine. Like you keep thinking that you have to shift gears but there aren't any more. Charlie was wearing a blue seersucker suit and had a little porkpie hat perched on the back of his head. Now and then the lenses of his glasses would catch the morning sun and sparkle. As for me, I was feeling a little ragged after a night in the slammer and I needed a shave.

We had left Mrs. Jennifer Holcomb-Smith outside city hall. She gave me her card and said she would be in Saratoga for the entire month of August. At first I thought she was making a pass, but it was nothing like that. She was curious about Fleshpot and curious about what might happen. Even so I found myself wondering if I could throw over the Queen of Softness for a woman with a bunch of millions in the bank. It was a moral struggle and I had to call a truce with myself before I came up with any hard answers.

We were on our way to the sales paddock to talk to Henry O'Leary, the agent who had sold Fleshpot for the original owner, Sycamore Farms in Kentucky. Although I had talked to him on the phone, I had never seen him in person. I don't believe we asked ourselves what we were doing. Butterworth's death had affected us so strongly that neither of us wondered what right we had to stick our noses in. We were detectives. Charlie was the boss and I was his trusty assistant. Consequently, we were detecting.

Charlie parked in front of the Pavilion and we got out. The place was almost deserted since the sales were over and the flat track races weren't due to start for another three hours. It was another sunny August morning with a smell of horses on the air. Now and then I heard a whinny. Birds were doing whatever birds do in late summer.

As we were walking between the Pavilion and the Fasig-Tipton offices who should come hurrying out of the Pavilion but Ms. Fletcher in a nice summer dress and her blond hair nailed in place. She gawked at me like a bunny might look up at a descending bald eagle.

"Boo!" I said.

"I thought you were in jail," she said, stepping back to the doorway and getting ready to run.

"There's no jail in Saratoga that can hold Vic Plotz," I told her.

Behind me I could hear Charlie sigh. "He was released for lack of evidence."

Ms. Fletcher stared at him as if to indicate that she couldn't believe it to be true. She was sure there must be tons of evidence. Her doubts made her look a trifle pop-eyed.

"If I don't get my check today," I told her, "Then I'll have to start work again." Even though the yearling sales were over, Fasig-Tipton would be selling horses of racing age and two-year-olds in training during the next week.

Ms. Fletcher's face lost a tad of its color. "I'll write up a check right away, Mr. Plotz."

Having spread this good cheer, I led Charlie on toward Barn Three West, where O'Leary was stabling his horses.

"Has it ever occurred to you," asked Charlie, "that there is no future in making people dislike you?"

"Now and then I wonder about that," I said. "The trouble is that the alternative just isn't any fun."

We were passing the Pinkerton office and I glanced inside. Talking to a couple of Pinkertons—deep in conversation, as they like to say—was Ron Novack, the no-neck copper.

"Look who's there," I said.

Charlie had already noticed him. "We can't waste any time."

"Feets don't fail me now," I said.

Henry O'Leary was a tall tweedy guy with a wing of graying brown hair across his high forehead whose major sadness in this life was that he hadn't been born in Dorset or Sussex or the Cotswolds or even Yorkshire. Every pore in his body yearned to be British. I bet even his underwear was imported. Maybe he was forty-five.

He was in the process of getting a buy-back ready to send down to Kentucky: a bay colt that hadn't made the price that the owner thought he could get and so they would try the September yearling sales in Lexington. Most of his other horses had already been shipped out to their new owners. The ringer that had been swapped for Fleshpot was being driven back to Saratoga and should arrive early in the afternoon. I felt sorry for the animal: it was the horse nobody wanted.

I don't know if O'Leary was in a hurry or didn't like questions or had a guilty conscience or had been warned off by the cops, but once Charlie had identified himself, O'Leary treated him like a stray case of the pox.

"I have absolutely nothing to say to you," he told us. He was about six inches taller than either of us and he stared down as if from a great height.

"Have you seen Rolf Macklin since Tuesday night?" asked Charlie.

"This is absolutely none of your business," said O'Leary.

"What about his cousin, Harry? Is he around?"

"I absolutely refuse to speak to you."

I tugged on O'Leary's tweedy sleeve. "How many times do you figure you say 'absolutely' in the course of a single day?"

O'Leary stared at me, opened his mouth, then abruptly closed it. He had some fine choppers.

"A man has been killed," said Charlie.

"I am very sorry about that," said O'Leary, who didn't look particularly sorry, "but presumably the police are investigating." He went back to giving directions to a groom about the bay colt. It was one of those situations where you want to kick a person, but you know you can't.

Charlie gave me a nod, then walked over to the little office. I toddled along behind. He opened the screen door and stepped inside. Over his shoulder I could see Jerry Pennyfeather fussing with some papers at his desk.

"Excuse me," said Charlie. "Could you give me Rolf and Harry Macklin's home address in Kingston?"

Pennyfeather looked up at him. The bangs of his black hair evenly bisected his forehead. I wondered what he saw when he looked at himself in the mirror. A handsome guy? A guy with a distinguished haircut that he vaguely remembered seeing on somebody important?

"Who are you?" said Pennyfeather. He didn't ask who I was because he thought he already knew. He just glared at me.

Charlie showed him his ID. "We're investigating the death of Paul Butterworth."

"On whose authority?"

"We've been retained by his family."

Charlie likes his little lie, but Pennyfeather wasn't going to take the hook.

"Beat it," he said.

"When did you last see them?" asked Charlie.

"I said, beat it," said Pennyfeather and he returned to fussing with his papers.

Then a voice behind us joined in with some more friendly remarks. "What the hell are you guys doing here?"

It was Ron Novack and another copper.

"Hey, it's No-neck Novack himself," I said.

"You break out of jail?" he asked me crossly. Novack was wearing a khaki suit and looked like a solid rectangle with a pimple on top. He has short hair to remind his interlocutors of his military background. Each strand looks stiff.

"Nope," I said. "Peterson put me back on the street."

Novack was staring at Charlie. He doesn't like him but he is also wary of him. "You got a client?" he asked.

"Maybe," said Charlie.

"Look," said Novack. "Saratoga's working on this, the state cops are working on this and an FBI guy is driving up from Albany. What do you think you're going to do?"

"I wanted to talk to Harry or Rolf Macklin," said Charlie.

"There aren't any Macklins," said Novack. "It was a fake name. They've disappeared. We're going to have over fifty professionals working on this. You'll do nothing but get in the way."

It occurred to me that with all his pumping iron, Novack was trying to turn himself into a wall: a big brick barricade. Like right now he looked like a wall, an obstacle between us and whatever we wanted to know. Not only that but he liked being a wall. It was his life's work.

"So you mind if I ask some questions?" said Charlie.

"None of this is your business, and if you interfere with us, I'll slap a charge on you."

"Do you have any leads on the Macklins?" asked Charlie.

"What did I just say?" said Novack. He flexed his shoulders and I heard a creaking noise. Pennyfeather was still someplace behind us in the office. O'Leary was leading the bay colt around the corner of the barn.

"Let's go, Victor," said Charlie.

"Vic," I reminded him.

We walked back toward the Pavilion. I felt an itch between my shoulder blades as if Novack was staring at us.

"Now what?" I asked Charlie.

"I want some names and phone numbers."

Charlie led the way back to the Fasig-Tipton sales offices across from the walking ring. The room was empty except for a woman behind the counter. Charlie gave her a big smile, commented on the beautiful weather, expressed regret that the sales were nearly over, then asked her who had bought Hip Fifty-seven. I had already told him it was Henrietta Farms in Oxbridge, Kentucky, but he wanted more than that.

"Who signed the purchase form?" asked Charlie.

The woman looked at a computer monitor. "George Slavino." She was a redhead in her thirties with a friendly smile. It had been so long since I had been smiled at that I almost thought there was something wrong with her face.

"Is he the agent for Henrietta Farms?"

"That's right."

"Did he also take possession of the horse?"

"He picked him up on Wednesday and transferred him to a trucking firm. They should be almost back to Kentucky by now," said the woman.

Fat lot you know, I said to myself.

"Do you have the name of anyone at Sycamore Farms?"

"Mrs. Roberta Fielding, she's the owner."

"Has she sold horses here before?"

"Oh yes, for years. She used to bring her horses up here herself but she's getting older now and she's retained an agent for the past four or five summers."

"Always O'Leary?"

"I believe so."

"And Slavino has been working as an agent for some time?"

The woman nodded, then touched her red hair. "At least since I've been here, and that's 1985."

"What happened to that black colt that got loose Tuesday night?" asked Charlie.

"It was scratched. Probably it's still around. The agent's name is Floyd Oliver."

Charlie wrote down the names and phone numbers. "Thank you," he told the woman. "You've been very helpful."

We walked across to the barn that had the Fasig-Tipton executive offices on the second floor. "You have any specific ideas?" I asked.

"Not yet," said Charlie.

We climbed the stairs to the second floor and Charlie found the Brit who was the announcer at the auction and who was also the company's director of marketing. His name was Patrick Sawyer, a blondish guy born to wear suits and ties.

"Legally the horse belongs to Henrietta Farms," said Sawyer

in response to a question of Charlie's, "unless it can be proved that the horse they bought right there in the Pavilion was not Hip Fifty-seven."

"So who takes the loss?" asked Charlie.

"Presumably Fasig-Tipton insurance. They provide coverage from the fall of the hammer."

"And who owns the ringer?" I asked.

"That," said Sawyer, "must still be decided."

I liked Sawyer. He had what they used to call manners, but what nowadays they call attitudes. Although he must have been thrown for a loop by the possibility of a theft right out of the sales paddock, he understood it was more important to keep his cool and remain a gentleman.

"Don't you feel guilty that you don't have enough guards to keep horses from being stolen?" I asked, just to needle him.

"We certainly can't turn the sales paddock into an armed camp," he said. "If the board decides that we need more guards, then we shall hire them."

As we made our way back downstairs, we met No-neck Novack on his way up.

"What did I tell you?" asked Novack.

"We've been good," I said.

The word "baleful" is a word I like, coming from the Icelandic word *bal,* meaning funeral pyre. That was the kind of look that Novack gave us: a funeral pyre sort of look.

We walked back into the sales paddock, looking for the agent Floyd Oliver. He was in his office doing the crossword. He was an old guy with about three lonely strands of hair on his shiny dome who had probably been coming up to Saratoga for fifty years.

"A groom, Kenny Maletti, was holding on to the black colt, Hip One Sixty-four. He said he just took off." Oliver didn't seem to mind talking to us. He was mystified and people who are mystified like to share their mystification, unless they are cops of course.

And Kenny Maletti told us: "One moment he was standing there, the next moment he gave a scream and was gone."

Maletti was in his mid-twenties and wore khakis and a blue golfing shirt. We stood by the black colt's stall, peering in at him. In the dim light, he was almost invisible except for the white bandages around his front ankles.

"Was anyone else around?" asked Charlie.

"Yeah, there were people. That colt that was sold for half a million had just gone by. Then my horse went crazy. I mean, he was fine before and he's been fine since."

"Maybe it was indigestion," I said.

A few minutes later we walked back to Charlie's car. Charlie said, "Maybe someone jabbed the horse with a pin or an ice pick, maybe he got shot with a pellet gun, maybe he got touched with a cattle prod."

"Whatever it was," I said, "he didn't like it." I looked over to the Fasig-Tipton parking lot and saw that Paul Butterworth's lime-green Volkswagen had been taken away. Presumably, the state coppers were checking it for clues.

"I bet it was a cattle prod," said Charlie. He took out his keys and opened the front door of the Mazda.

"So what are we going to do now?" I asked as I crawled into the front seat, trying not to bump any of the prize flesh against the car's sharp edges.

"I think we'll talk to Arnold Steinfeld."

"My nemesis," I said.

The lawyer had his offices right downtown on Broadway just north of the post office. In fact, I could see his windows from my apartment in the Algonquin. He had interviewed me—not to say grilled me—in the presence of my own lawyer about a month before, concerning the funds which he felt I had ripped off from his client, Mrs. Ross. He would ask something and my own lawyer, Arthur Woodward, would say, "You don't have to answer that." And it seemed to me that these lawyers and all the other lawyers were trying to create a situation where they became the intermediaries in all the world's transactions. Like you want to give the love of your life a little carnal and cohabitational squeeze, so you send your lawyer to talk to her lawyer. You want to buy some Juicyfruit gum so you ask your lawyer if it would be a good idea. Lawyers want to become a kind of human condom purifying all affairs, all transactions, all communication. Soon schizophrenics will need lawyers just to talk to themselves.

Steinfeld was a little bald guy who smelled of money. Charlie knew him and didn't have anything in particular against him, even though Steinfeld had been making my life a misery. Some friend, right? Steinfeld's secretary kept us waiting for about ten minutes, then ushered us into his office: glass-topped tables and desks and chromium Swedish chairs. It had all the warmth of a freezer chest.

"And why should I talk to you?" asked Steinfeld. His tone was more curious than rude.

Charlie was deferential. "We both liked Paul Butterworth and we worry that his death might be pushed aside because of the money involved: the fact that a half-million-dollar horse has been stolen. I just want to make sure that Butterworth wasn't doing any other job for you. Possibly his death had nothing to do with the stolen horse."

Steinfeld was silent for a moment, then he took out a white handkerchief and patted his brow, even though the office was cool. We were all standing up in the middle of the room. "He was a nice boy. No, he wasn't doing any other work for me. And I certainly wouldn't have had him making a nuisance of himself with Mr. Plotz if I had thought he might be in danger."

"I'm sure of that," said Charlie. "Had he been working for you long?"

"No, no, he only graduated from Skidmore in May. He came here looking for some work and said he wanted to be a private investigator. Actually, I was hoping to persuade him to go back to school, get a master's or Ph.D. He was the kind of person you worried about. Do you have any idea why he was killed?"

"I guess," said Charlie, "that he saw the two horses being swapped. It was during that time when a horse had gotten loose in the paddock. He was following Victor, then must have lost him in the commotion."

Steinfeld gave me a cold look as if I was in some way responsible.

"Hey," I said, "I liked him too."

"I feel terrible about it," said Steinfeld. "I've talked to his parents in Connecticut. The funeral will be on Monday and I intend to drive down."

I discovered in myself a desire to go to the funeral as well, even though I doubted that my Yugo would make the trip. Charlie and Steinfeld talked a little more about death—the great dissolver, the big troublemaker, the guy who crashes life's party.

A little later I went back to my apartment to shower, shave and change my clothes. I felt beat from a night of lousy sleep and I felt beat because of what had happened to Butterworth. It must be something in our psychology that makes us think that people are so permanent, because with no more than a click they can cease to be there.

Because I have unfortunate sentimental tendencies which I attempt to suppress, I called Butterworth's phone number just so I could hear his voice on the answering machine. Once again I heard him reading that poem called "Likes." He had a slightly high voice as if his testicles had not as yet descended all the way and he tended to clip his words as if he wanted to get them out into the world as fast as possible. You could hear all his life in his voice: the insecurities that went along with being twenty-two and the attempt at a confidence which he hoped would someday replace those insecurities.

> *He's never understood the holy admonition*
> *About being a lily of the field—because he wouldn't*
> *Want to stay rooted to one place. He wants to clarify*
> *The concept of getting lost. This is my occupation,*
> *He thinks, shaking a stone from inside his boot.*
> *He likes to eat fungus and berries and the little apples*
> *The deer can't reach. He likes to walk through the rain*
> *And stand straight up in a grove of pines.*
> *He likes to strip off his clothes and sleep in the sun*
> *Or touch the petals where they rise. He says*
> *"Why not be pollen before we're dust."*

10

did not go to Paul Butterworth's funeral, for which I felt guilty. I decided I didn't want to see his parents and see their grief. Like it wasn't my fault he had been killed, but if he had never laid eyes on me, he would still be among the living. I imagined his parents looking at me and thinking those very thoughts.

But don't think I just sat around with my feet up. I became Charlie's trusted employee on the Fleshpot case. I followed him around and watched him ask a lot of questions. Not that it did us any good. The big trouble was that we didn't have access. The city cops wouldn't talk to us, the state cops wouldn't talk to us, the Pinkertons wouldn't talk to us, the FBI wouldn't talk to us, the investigation division of the Racing Association wouldn't talk to us. And when Charlie contacted the sellers, Sycamore Farms, and the buyers, Henrietta Farms, and the sellers' agent, Henry O'Leary, and the buyers' agent, George Slavino, he received a range of responses from rudeness to silence. Even one of the few nice people, Mrs. Roberta Fielding of Sycamore Farms, explained that she had been asked by the authorities not to talk to anyone outside the case. For crying out loud, we were getting most of our information from the newspapers!

The *Daily Racing Form* did an article on the ringer. The blood didn't match up, of course, and the white blaze on his forehead turned out to be dye, just like I said. Neither the ringer's blood nor his nighteyes were on record, meaning he was nothing special. He was just a pretty colt with nothing else to recommend him. I felt sorry for him. Yesterday a star, tomorrow a stable pony.

The *Saratogian* had several articles about Butterworth's murder. He had been killed by a blow to the head from a blunt object about eleven forty-five Tuesday night and then, at some point, his body had been taken out to Lake Saratoga and tossed in the water. A chain, taken from one of the gates at the sales paddock, had been wrapped around his waist to hold him down. The fisherman who had snagged him must have thought he had caught a whale. The guy had reeled in the body very slowly, then had seen a hand coming up through the water.

The article also said that two grooms, hired by Henry O'Leary for the sales, were missing. It didn't give their names or describe them. Personally, I couldn't see the Macklins killing anybody. They were nice enough guys and although they might steal a horse, bloodshed seemed a little excessive. But I figured I was wrong. Or maybe one of them had tapped Butterworth on the head and had used more force than he intended. Whoops, they had a corpse. It didn't make it any better, but at least it wasn't murder in cold blood.

Fasig-Tipton also determined that the horse which had been sold in the Pavilion was Fleshpot, which I could have told them, because hadn't the horse taken a bite out of his handler's backside? But consequently the buyer took the loss, or rather the buyer's insurance company, which was also Fasig-Tipton. So Mrs. Roberta Fielding got her half million, less commissions and taxes, and Henrietta Farms was paid off by the insurance company. Even Henrietta Farms' agent, George Slavino, got his commission.

Charlie called the Fasig-Tipton insurance company to see if they wanted to hire a reliable investigator. I was touched by his innocent persistence. He genuinely thought they might want to hire him. They were not entirely rude, but they made it clear that they already had lots of investigators.

So there we were, all dressed up and no place to go. On Monday morning, the 15th, I stopped by Charlie's office for coffee and a couple of bagels, which I supplied. He had his feet up on the desk and was reading the *Racing Form*. There was a lot of noise from the street, cars and honking and people calling to one another. In August, Saratoga Springs swells to three times its normal size and by late morning there is a long traffic jam on the thirty miles of the Northway between the Albany and Saratoga exits. Like hundreds of state employees take their two-week vacations in half days so they can get four weeks at the track. The smart people who are not keen on racing rent their places through an agency for a bundle and take what amounts to a free vacation. And me too, before the stock market crash of 1994 I did that as well.

"What I don't understand," said Charlie, thinking out loud, "is that the ringer would have been discovered in any case. By Friday he would have reached Henrietta Farms and presumably he would have been checked over by a vet. By today they would have given him a complete physical and the different blood would have been discovered. So maybe the deception would have lasted five or six days, no more."

Charlie's sparse gray hair was sticking up straight on the top of his head. It always does that when he thinks hard. He was wearing his blue seersucker suit. Actually, I think he has several of them.

"So the people who stole the horse needed five free days," continued Charlie. "What could they do in that time?"

"Get the horse out of the country?" I suggested.

"That's right." He looked pleased with me.

"But how could they race him?"

"Maybe they have no intention of racing him. Maybe they would only use him for stud."

"But wouldn't his blood cause a problem there too? All that stuff has got to be on computers."

"Sure, but it's not as systematized in some of the third world countries as it is here or in Europe. And think of the progeny. Although they might not be superstars, they certainly could be better than anybody expected. Asia, Africa, South America—the horse might be anywhere."

"So you think the Macklins did this?"

"I can't believe they did it by themselves. I managed to talk to one of O'Leary's grooms at the Parting Glass. He said that although they claimed to be from Kingston, he didn't think they were from the east, but maybe that's hindsight. But he said they didn't know any of the usual place-names. Even Poughkeepsie they hadn't heard of. So maybe they were from out west."

"They had that healthy California look," I said.

"I should think they would turn up eventually," said Charlie. "Although if Butterworth hadn't been killed and if the swap hadn't been discovered so quickly, they might have just faded away."

"Where do you think they are now?" I asked.

"Depends whether they have Fleshpot. After all, the cops must have put out an APB on a chestnut colt sometime Thursday morning. They're probably stopping horse trailers all over the country. So either the people who stole Fleshpot had already delivered him, or they're lying low."

"Playing possum," I said. "I've done that myself."

■ ■ ■

There was also the problem of my employment, since my job at the Humphrey S. Finney Pavilion had come to an end. That was another of our topics of conversation Monday morning. After half a dozen possibilities were rejected (dishwasher, street sweeper, crossing guard), Charlie suggested that he call his mother at the Hotel Bentley. I didn't so much swallow my pride as shove it down my throat with a stick. What else could I do? I had to eat, didn't I? So Charlie called her. Listening to Charlie's half of the conversation as he talked to his mother set my teeth on edge.

"I'm certain he'll apologize for what he did before," Charlie was saying. "He terribly regretted getting the hotel in trouble. . . . Do I think he has turned over a new leaf? Really, Mother, you would hardly know him." This went on for a while, ending with the statement: "I'll send him over."

"At least you didn't tell her that I'd started going to church."

"I was about to. Luckily, she was in a forgiving mood."

"Well," I said, "I'm grateful even though I don't like it."

Charlie nodded sympathetically. "I've been there myself."

Mabel Bradshaw was a lady somewhere in her mid-seventies, although she didn't look it. She had more paint on her than a Picasso, more supporting struts and trusses than the Brooklyn Bridge. Seeing her, one would never guess that she had spent nearly forty years as a hash-house waitress. But there's a kind of person they have around Saratoga, I guess they have them all over, who uses his or her spare nickels and dimes to buy part of a horse: sometimes a racehorse, sometimes a trotter. These aren't stakes horses and most of them stay only a few hops ahead of the dog-food factory. As an investment, owning a chunk of a horse is probably a little better than the lottery. But then, bingo, one summer Mabel Bradshaw made a bundle on her nag, and then bingo again, she increased her nest egg in Atlantic City, and the next thing you know she's a grand dame with a hotel. Then she started hanging out with the ballet people and the theater people and at the end of every September she took off for southern France for seven months. And the hash-house waitress? All trace is erased. Not even the FBI could give you a better new identity.

I had my interview in her suite on the second floor of the hotel: red flocked wallpaper and Tiffany lamps. Like I wouldn't dream of calling her Mabel to her face anymore. She was wearing a kind of old-timey Victorian dress—a flowing emerald-green skirt and a severe white bodice that buttoned at the neck—to go with her old-timey Victorian hotel. She sat on a chaise lounge covered with some dark-colored satiny material and I stood.

"Tell me, Victor," she said, "I gather you have been driving a Mercedes." She was smoking a cigarette in a long holder and she waved it at me.

"Yes, until recently."

"How did you like it?"

"A wonderful car, ma'am. Rode like an angel."

"And Cadillacs, how do you feel about those?"

"They've come a long way. Today's Cadillac is very competitive with the Mercedes."

"And BMWs."

"Another fine car."

"And Jaguars?"

"Not a car for the long haul, but a pleasure while it lasts."

Now this was exciting talk. It was clear that she had in mind some executive position which would come with a big car. I mean, not only did Mabel Bradshaw own this fancy hotel in Saratoga, but she had opened another in Lake George and a third over by Tanglewood in the Berkshires. She was plainly in need of executives and she couldn't have one of her executives driving a Yugo. I didn't blame her. Obviously, if she was going to hire class, she would have to give that class a classy car.

"Personally," I said, "I think I would look best in a nice red Porsche, or perhaps a dark gray Aston Martin to match the color of my hair. Although I must say, I can also see myself in a lilac-colored Morgan."

Mabel Bradshaw looked at me and blinked, slowly. "I should say, Mr. Plotz, that the job I have in mind for you is parking garage attendant. You would drive the guests' cars from the front of the hotel to the back. And of course you would have a uniform. But be of good cheer. It too is gray and would match your hair."

Slam-dunked.

So that was how I spent the week, driving rich people's cars from the front of the hotel to the back or from the back of the hotel to the front. Sometimes I got a five-dollar tip. For a while, I had a little fun squealing, "Sho' boss, ri' away, boss!" But then the manager told me I was being politically incorrect. "Impossible," I told him. "I've voted Democratic all my life."

Of course, I called Steinfeld and told him that once again I had found humble employment, but that I might be able to save ten to fifteen smackers a week to give to Mrs. Ross to help make up for the thousands which she claimed I had lost in the stock market crash. You see how these people only think of themselves? What about me? What about my great losses?

I did not work the weekend. That was fine with me, except that Mabel Bradshaw made it clear to me that I wasn't important enough to work the weekend when her really classy guests would be arriving. I asked her if she had retained an Equity actor who had become famous on *Gunsmoke,* or perhaps she had hired Big Bird from *Sesame Street.* This did not go down well. Why is it that as people get richer, their sense of humor decreases?

"You know who's got a reservation at the hotel this week-end?" Charlie asked me on Friday.

"Gunga Din?"

"Jim Lehrer."

"You mean the ex–Harvard teacher who used to sing those funny songs about Boy Scouts?"

"I mean Jim Lehrer of *The MacNeil-Lehrer News Hour* on TV."

"I don't watch TV, that's what I got a vibrator for. If more people had vibrators, there'd be a whole lot less TV."

Charlie let that pass. "Maybe you'll drive his car," he said. "I bet he drives a Mercedes."

"An unkind cut, Charlie. I used to drive one myself."

On Saturday I took the Queen of Softness to the track. The plan was to meet up with Charlie and Janey Burris and have lunch in the clubhouse. The weather was cool, somewhere in the sixties, and the sun was bright: a cloudless blue sky. Perfect track weather—we thought that and so did fifty thousand other people eager to lose their bucks on the pretty horses. By one o'clock we were happily strolling around. There are certain decorative bits of business at the track that make the blood beat fast. Like when the bugler blares out the call to the horses or when the guy in the paddock says "Riders up!" and all the jocks hop on their nags. Then as the horses amble out to the track, people along the white rail fence call to the jockeys, "Let's go, Julie, I'm with you." "Bring her home, Jorge." Or sometimes they aren't so pleasant. "Where the hell were you last time, Bailey?"

My lady, the Queen of Softness, has a forty-five-inch bust and those are the numbers I always bet for the daily double: four and five. And believe me, if Cupid truly existed those numbers would turn up winners, but so far they haven't. Rosemary is a lady who prefers solid colors to patterns and she is partial to satin which she buys by the half mile and makes into gowns (don't call them dresses, she'd get mad). On this Saturday she wore a yellow satin gown with a matching parasol and décolletage of sufficient dimensions to accommodate the *Andrea Doria*. Charlie had exchanged his seersucker suit for a light blue one. Janey wore a pretty blue polka-dot dress but she must have felt a little shabby compared to Rosemary because she kept staring at her. I wore a dove-gray suit.

I had the feeling that Charlie and Janey had been quarreling because they were a bit stiff with one another, but Rosemary took their arms and led them to the clubhouse where we all got our hands stamped for the ultraviolet. A few years ago a fellow couldn't get into the clubhouse without a jacket and a tie, but the racing people have found those rules not cost-productive and they were tossed on the trash heap. Like what's more important, a few extra bucks or class? Basically, the business of Saratoga is not the propagation of the Sport of Kings but to rake in the shekels as fast as possible, so any little thing that gets in the way—like a necktie—must be asked to leave.

We had a table reserved right above the finish line and we took our seats just as the first race ended and the number twelve horse galloped to victory to the happy bellowing of about ten thousand fans. So much for the Queen of Softness's bust.

As the crowd quieted, I said, "I guess I should have bet the length of my . . ."

"Victor!" interrupted Rosemary.

"Forearm," I said.

Stuffy waiters in white jackets came and went. We consulted our menus and ordered: veal piccata, poached baby salmon, medallions of lamb, duckling Alsace—like we were only eating children on that day. The restaurant is steeply tiered with tables upon tables. We looked down upon the well-dressed and wealthy and they looked down upon us, although I must say that the fellows sitting above Rosemary's décolletage made a little fuss.

"Perhaps I should wear a bib," she said.

Rosemary won a hundred smackers on the second race on a nag called My Mother's Blue Eyes. It had been the color that had convinced her. I went to gather her winnings and place our bets for the third race. Charlie plunked ten dollars on a filly called Lonely in Love, which I thought was a bad sign. Janey Burris wasn't betting. I put down twenty on a big roan named Beef Torpedo.

When I sat back down, I could see that Charlie was all excited. "Victor, Victor, I just saw him."

I immediately assumed that he meant one of the Macklins, Rolf or Harry.

"Which one?" I asked, looking around.

My question seemed to stump him. "Which? I mean Jim Lehrer, the guy on TV."

"Aha, the newshound. Why don't you see if he has any tips for the fourth race. Personally, I think Metal Magic looks good."

Janey was excited too. "He's sitting right over there," she said.

I looked over at a table where a handsome guy with woodchuck eyes was sitting with an attractive middle-aged woman with short brown hair and some kind of red, white and blue sash over her shoulder which looked a little ragged. There was also another guy with a black eye patch. The fellow with the woodchuck eyes was staring at his program, presumably reading it, and nibbling on a pencil eraser.

"I used to know a guy with a glass eye," I said. "Every now and then he would replace it with a big yellow cat's-eye marble and scare the bejesus out of people. Waitresses, mostly. He got them to drop their trays."

I was about to go on when I saw a familiar face just beyond their table. It was Jerry Pennyfeather with his Moe of the Three Stooges haircut.

I don't think Charlie saw him. He was too caught up with

Lehrer and with asking Janey if she thought it would be okay to ask Lehrer to sign his program. He and Janey were all friendly now, as if Mr. Lehrer's presence had let them forget their differences.

Pennyfeather was with a blonde in a flowery peach-colored dress and a showy hat. They were both bent over a bright green tip sheet which they had probably bought from some tout at the gate. I was surprised that Pennyfeather would throw away his money so easily. I mean, these touts write fiction like Stephen King writes fiction. Pennyfeather had his hand on the nape of his lady's neck and was massaging it slowly as they made their calculations. Then he stood up and headed off to make a bet.

I got a little idea and asked Rosemary to come with me. She couldn't hurry so well in her high heels. The betting window was on the next floor and I told Rosemary what I wanted as we climbed the stairs. When she walks her platinum locks make gestures of farewell to the people she leaves behind. But I don't think Charlie saw us go. He was still watching Jim Lehrer, trying to figure out what horse he was going to plonk his money on.

Rosemary took her place in line behind Pennyfeather. About five or six people were in front of them. Rosemary was taller than Pennyfeather and her breasts reached out toward his shoulders. He was nattily dressed in a blue suit. Rosemary bumped him.

"Oh, Mr. Pennyfeather," she said. "You're just the man I wanted to see. Where are those wonderful boys, Rolf and Harry Macklin? I owe them money."

Pennyfeather looked like he had been sapped from behind. He spun around so quickly that he nearly stuck his nose in Rosemary's décolletage. "Money?" he asked. He took a step backward and stepped on the foot of the next person in line: a big man who said, "Hey!"

"Rolf and Harry gave me a tip on a horse," beamed Rosemary. "And it won! So I owe them each fifty dollars."

Pennyfeather stepped back again in another direction. He seemed to have a terror of being poked by Rosemary's breasts. You've heard of the third degree? Her knockers were the fourth and fifth degrees. "A tip?" he said, probably thinking of the proverbial iceberg.

"I told them I'd give them ten percent of my winnings. Where are they?" She waggled a little.

Pennyfeather took hold of himself. "Maybe I can give the money to them . . ." he began, but then he caught sight of me. "You son of a gun!"

"So you know where they are?" I asked brightly.

There were a lot of people around us waiting to place a bet. Let me say that a man or woman getting ready to put money down on a nag absolutely hates the slightest interference.

"Hey, come on," barked a bald guy.

"Let's get the line moving," complained a lady.

"To hell with you," said Pennyfeather. He turned back to the line. Only one person was before him at the window.

"So where are Harry and Rolf?" I asked. "And where's Flesh-pot?"

Pennyfeather bet an exacta for the fifth race: four and five. I was so stunned that he was betting Rosemary's bust line, the same bust line that had cost me money on the double, that I was for a moment at a loss for words. My only thought was to get into line and bet the same numbers.

"The cops told me not to talk to you," said Pennyfeather, making his bet.

Now it was my turn to be impatient. Pennyfeather took his ticket from the clerk and scurried off, not looking at me but knowing I was there. Instead of going after him and making his life a misery, I stepped to the window in order to plonk fifty bucks on the four and the five. I was planning to make a bundle.

So you see how it goes: one half dream, the other half harsh
reality. And without the dream, how could we do anything? It's
the dream of better times that lets us sleep at night and keeps our
thoughts buoyant during the day. Going back downstairs, I
checked out one of the television monitors and discovered that
the four and five exacta would pay off a couple of grand. Rosemary and me already began spending the money. We'd go to the
Cape for the first two weeks in September. We'd live off the fat
of the land.

Sad to say, neither the four nor the five even showed. In fact,
they crossed the finish line at least five minutes after the other
horses, hobbling, moaning and carrying on. I wondered if Pennyfeather hadn't steered me wrong on purpose. Two weeks on
the Cape drifted away like yesterday's perfume. As we walked
back up from the finish line, Charlie and Janey came hurrying
toward us. Charlie was holding up his program.

"Look what I have," he said.

I figured he had won the exacta and felt a soupçon of anger
for my pal. But he wasn't talking about horses. He'd gotten Jim
Lehrer to sign his program. I looked at him for a moment: a
cheerful guy with a round face and bright blue eyes staring
proudly at a wrinkled piece of paper. His plaid porkpie hat
looked ready to slide off the back of his head and his bifocals had
thumb smudges on them, but he was happy. He had even forgotten to place a bet.

For the next two hours I searched all over for Pennyfeather.
Maybe I walked twenty miles. But there was no trace of him. He
had skedaddled. Perhaps it was a clue, I thought.

11

August wound to its conclusion with one pretty day after another. I went to the track a few more times. Maybe I finished the season about a hundred bucks ahead. Rosemary won a couple of thousand but she always does. Charlie and Janey continued their strained conversations with her wanting to put their relationship "on a more solid footing" as she called it, and Charlie not wanting to, or rather, he thought it was solid enough. Charlie was a great defender of the status quo. That's what being a detective is all about: one becomes the enemy of change and entropy. Like James Bond, right? He wanted a world which didn't mess with his fast cars, fast girls, pricey wines or his cigars. And when something tried to interfere with James Bond, he stomped it. Maybe Charlie was a little like that.

I continued to park cars for the Hotel Bentley and I pretty much behaved myself, although one Friday evening I drove a guest's Maserati an extra couple of miles, which caused me to get yelled at. In September, however, the Bentley winds down pretty quick. The track is closed, schools have started, and after Labor Day I was no longer needed. This was not as bad as it might have been because Lawyer Steinfeld was no longer breathing hot and heavy down my neck. Instead of words like "fraud" and "criminal mischief" being bandied about, there were words like "unfortunate circumstances" and "regrettable errors."

As a result I began a little buying and selling, in a small way, and I even got myself another cellular phone, a better one this time. My fax and my modem began to crank up again. I walked a little faster, held my head up a little higher. Cattle futures looked good once again, hog bellies bubbled.

But I was circumspect. I kept the Yugo. No longer did I have cronies call me in public places like the Parting Glass so I could bellow out questions about the Japanese stock market. The Carnegies, Rockefellers, Vanderbilts—in order to become rich you have to be sneaky. Circumspect, like I say. It would be hard work but if I didn't learn to hide my light under a bushel, then my light would find itself hidden away in jail.

Although life was picking up, I couldn't get Paul Butterworth out of my mind. I kept seeing lime-green Volkswagen Beetles out of the corner of my eye. I kept hearing him reading that damn poem on his answering machine. Toward the end of August I called his number again and a tape-recorded voice told me that his line had been disconnected. That's right, I thought, the ultimate disconnection.

A couple of times I stopped by police headquarters but I never got to see Peterson or No-neck Novack. Peterson's retirement was set for October 1st and considering the preparations you would have thought that the Pope himself was coming to town. Peterson had been police chief, or Commissioner of Public Safety, for twenty-nine years, and that number was being bandied about as if there was something sacred about it: like the number of years the Jews had been in Egypt or the years that Ted Williams led in home runs. Actually it wasn't exactly true that I didn't see Peterson. I happened to run into him one day as I was leaving police headquarters and he was coming in.

"Just make certain, Plotz," he said, "that you have absolutely nothing to do with my retirement parade."

"Parade?" I said.

"No comment," he said. And he hurried upstairs.

As for Butterworth's murder, I was told by the desk sergeant that there were no new developments but an arrest was expected imminently. The FBI wouldn't talk to me and the Racing Association wouldn't say anything about Fleshpot.

Charlie had been poking around and knew slightly more than I did, but what he knew was that nobody knew anything. As far as he could see, there was nothing left to be done.

"There's no trace of those Macklin cousins and no trace of the horse," he told me.

We were sitting in his office. It was the very beginning of September and a cool breeze was coming through the window. I was struck by how quiet the streets were after the hustle and bustle of August. Oh, happy somnolent Saratoga once again.

"So what should we do?" I asked.

"Nothing. Or rather, just wait. Maybe something will turn up." He shrugged and stuck out his lower lip at me to indicate perplexity and dissatisfaction.

"I've never been a patient guy," I told him.

"You surprise me," he said.

One day at the track at the end of August I had happened to see Henry O'Leary in his British tweeds. I was by myself and I followed him around for a while. I suppose it was possible that he could have stolen Fleshpot, since the Macklins worked for him. The trouble was that I couldn't think what to ask him except: "Did you steal the horse and kill Paul Butterworth?" Somehow that struck me as insufficiently subtle.

But after a while I cozied up to him at a bar in the clubhouse and after saying, "Hey, remember me?" and watching his eyes glaze over, I said, "Did you ever get a line on where that ringer came from?"

O'Leary looked down on me with a cool expression, or maybe it was no expression at all. He was wearing a nice summer wool sport coat and his binoculars were draped around his neck like a string of pearls. "I have absolutely no reason in the world to speak to you," he said.

"You have any tips on the fifth race?" I asked, hoping at least for a smidgin of something useful.

O'Leary had only picked up his drink, a dry martini, and drifted away.

But the question of the ringer stayed in my mind and a few days later I tracked down George Slavino, the agent who had bought Fleshpot for Henrietta Farms. I called him at his office in Newburgh.

"And who did you say you were?" he kept asking.

"Vic Corn, I'm a reporter up here for the *Union-Leader*. I was wondering about that ringer you got stuck with instead of Hip Fifty-seven in Saratoga."

"And why do you want to know?" Slavino had a gruff New York accent and sounded about as friendly as a Manhattan tow truck.

"Let's say it's an animal interest story that several hundred thousand capitol district residents are dying to learn the answer to."

"I don't know what happened to the horse," he said. "Technically, it belongs to the insurance company."

"You going down to the September sales in Lexington?" I asked. That was the September yearling sales that Fasig-Tipton would run from the 9th through the 11th.

"Sure. I mean, that's my business. What's that got to do with the ringer?"

"Well, I was wondering if you were worried about getting stuck with any more ringers."

"Look, buster, I didn't buy that ringer and I don't know anything about it, so if you don't mind . . ." There was a click. I told myself that I had found one more human being who wasn't destined to become a pal.

I was interested in the September sales, because Charlie had said that if anything was going to happen, it would most likely occur after the September sales took place. I don't know how he knew that. Maybe he thought that the person or persons who had swiped Fleshpot would try to unload him in Lexington on the sly. In any case, Charlie turned out to be right.

It was Thursday evening, the 22nd, and I was sitting at home solidifying my relationship with Moshe III, my cat: a little chin tickle, a little ear scratch. On Tuesday nights the Queen of Softness has a number of lady pals over to her place to discuss whatever ladies discuss when there are no men around. Charlie had taken Janey Burris over to his place for a special dinner with candles, trying to put the magic back in their relationship.

It was raining. One of those schizophrenic September nights which first feels like summer and then feels like fall. I had the living-room windows open and the long curtains blew into the room. It was about ten-fifteen. Now and then I would hear a car hiss past on Broadway. I was trying to read a book on the stock market but Moshe III was sitting on my lap and he kept standing up, turning around, tickling my nose with his tail, then settling down again. My CD player was playing a Gerry Mulligan and Stan Getz disc from the fifties: "Anything Goes" and "Too Close for Comfort." The notes of their two saxophones joined together like plump pastel ribbons making curlicues in the middle of the air. Some nights very long ago when I got off work from Schultz's Men's Furnishings in New York I used to stop by the Metropole to hear Cozy Cole slam-bang his way through a few tunes for the tourists. Then I'd take the subway back to Brooklyn where my wife would have cooked up corned beef and cabbage and my kid would be eager to show me his report card or something else exciting he had done in school. So you can see, listening to the music and scratching Moshe's ears, I had gotten myself into a melancholy mood.

When the knock came on the door, I was surprised, not just because of the lateness of the hour, but because the Algonquin has a buzzer system downstairs, and whoever this person was, he or she had either slipped into the building or was a neighbor. Neither possibility cheered me.

I dumped Moshe on the floor, stuck my reading glasses back in my breast pocket and headed for the door. I opened up and there was Harry Macklin, the older of the two cousins. He had a grin on his face but there was some uncertainty behind it.

"Remember me?" he asked.

"John Wilkes Booth?"

"Who?" He looked more uncertain and pushed back a strand of black hair that had fallen over his eye. He was wearing jeans, a dark sweatshirt and a jean jacket that was wet from the rain.

"Forget it. Where's Fleshpot?"

"That's what I wanted to talk to you about."

"How'd you get into the building?"

"I followed somebody else."

I thought how this was the guy who had supposedly murdered Paul Butterworth and how I was about to invite him into my apartment. But I couldn't see that he had any reason to scrag me and besides I wanted to know what was on his mind.

"Come on in," I said, then stepped aside to let him pass. His jeans were none too clean and I thought he smelled of horse. "You want a beer?" I asked.

"Sure," he said. "I'd like that."

So I went into the kitchen, opened the fridge and got myself a beer as well, Rolling Rocks all around, then I also got some crackers and cheese. When I returned to the living room, Harry Macklin was sitting on the couch scratching Moshe's ears.

I gave him the beer and put the crackers and cheese on the coffee table. "So I guess your name's not Harry Macklin."

"You can call me Bobby," he said. He drank some beer, then grabbed a couple of crackers.

"What's the last name? Shaftoe?"

He let that float by ungrasped. "Flynn," he said.

I sat down in the armchair across from him. "So where's Fleshpot?" I was trying to look cool, like nothing could rile me, but I could feel my heart beating fast.

Macklin, or Bobby, gave me another smile, the sort of smile that is designed to indicate that the person who is smiling is basically harmless. What bothered me was not the smile, but that Bobby also looked scared.

"The chestnut colt?" he asked. "They want to kill him."

"What?" I put down my beer.

Bobby grinned again, pleased to have my undivided attention. "Yeah," he said. "That's what I wanted to talk to you about. You see, the buy fell through and we're stuck with the horse. Then they thought they could sell him in Lex, but I guess that didn't work either, so now they want to put him down, that's the part that me and Josh don't like."

"Josh?"

"He's my cousin. The guy you knew as Rolf Macklin."

"Is he a Flynn as well?" I asked.

"That's right, our dads are brothers."

"Why don't we back up a little? Who's this 'they' you keep mentioning?"

Bobby kept bouncing his left knee up and down and looking around. Sometimes he would take a swig of beer, sometimes he would reach out to the cat.

"I'd rather not say who they are, or who he is, since that would only get me in worse trouble than I'm already putting myself." He grinned, probably proud of his syntax, then he pushed back his black hair again.

"Worse than murder?" I asked.

Well, that question seemed to tranquilize him quite nicely. His hand paused in midair over Moshe's furry dome. "What murder?" he asked.

"Paul Butterworth's murder."

Bobby's brow developed some creases. "Who's he?"

"He's a kid who got bashed on the head right about the time you swapped Fleshpot for the ringer. Then his body was thrown in the lake. The cops have a serious interest in this."

"Oh, Jesus," Bobby said softly.

"Did you hit him?"

Bobby got excited again. "Hit him? I didn't even know him!"

"You don't have to be introduced in order to kill a guy," I said helpfully.

"I mean, I didn't know anything about him!"

"The cops think that you and your cousin killed him because he caught you swapping the horses. If you're lucky you'll get off with second degree murder."

Bobby's eyes got a little bigger. "Jesus, I never laid eyes on him, neither did Josh. It must of been Pennyfeather. We knew nothing about it."

"Pennyfeather?" I asked.

"It was his scam. He arranged the thing with the ringer and got us in there to help." Bobby finished his beer and I went to get him another. He needed liquid solace.

"So it was Pennyfeather that arranged to steal Fleshpot?" I asked, handing him the Rolling Rock.

"That's right."

"And he had a buyer?"

Bobby Flynn took off his jean jacket and spread it out on the back of the couch to dry. "Some rich Chilean," he said. "We were supposed to truck the horse down to Miami on Friday after the sales, but suddenly the deal got canceled and we were stuck with the horse. I figured the news got out about the ringer a lot sooner than Pennyfeather had expected and the Chilean got cold feet. Pennyfeather said he'd find another buyer in Lex, but he hasn't been able to. So now he wants to kill the horse and Josh and me just can't stomach it. We got to kill it and bury it and go back to San Diego like nothing's happened."

"Killing a horse isn't as bad as killing a man," I said.

"Jesus, we didn't kill anybody."

"Was Pennyfeather working by himself?"

Bobby opened his mouth and shut it again. "I don't know. He's the only guy we've seen and we haven't seen much of him."

"Where are you keeping the horse?"

"Over in the next county."

"What's the town?"

"There's a tiny place called Shushan and a bigger place called Cambridge, but we're way out in the sticks. There aren't even any houses around. I drive into Cambridge for supplies. Shushan's good enough for cigarettes and beer." Bobby pushed up the sleeves of his sweatshirt. On his left forearm was a blue tattoo of a bird in flight, maybe a swallow.

"You in a barn?"

"An old mill. We got the horse and we have to keep him out of sight. Pennyfeather wouldn't give us a TV. We got some video games on an old computer. He also dumped off a big box of comics but we read them already. I mean, we'd of stuck it. We'd stay there another month if we had to. Pennyfeather promised us five grand each and maybe more, but we can't see killing the horse. I mean, he's a nice horse."

"Why'd you come to me?"

"We can't go to the cops and we don't know anyone else. You seemed friendly enough. You'd talked to us. The other day in Cambridge, I looked you up in the phone book and it gave this address. Josh and I have been discussing it. You're the only guy we know! If we can turn the horse over to you and maybe you can give us, say, five hundred bucks for doing this good deed, then we can take off and no one will find us. But we got to hurry because Pennyfeather wants to kill the horse now."

I thought about this. Unfortunately, I have to say that the chance of saving the horse, getting my name in the papers and outwitting the cops was a joyous prospect. Think of how rude all these guys had been: the city cops, the state cops, the FBI, the Pinkertons, the Racing Association. I wanted to have my mug next to Fleshpot's mug on the front page of the *Saratogian,* and maybe I could also scrounge up some official apologies. The trouble was the murder. Even if Harry and Rolf Macklin, or Bobby and Josh Flynn, knew nothing of it, they were still accomplices until a jury decided otherwise. And if I helped them escape, then I would be an accomplice as well.

"Five hundred bucks?" I said.

"We got no money. Maybe just a hundred between us. We got no way to get back to California."

"What about two hundred and fifty?" I said.

"It's a deal," said Bobby, sticking out his hand.

Well, I was in a pickle. My own partiality for striking a bargain had been my undoing. On the other hand, I could truly see my own picture in the *Saratogian* cheek to jowl with Fleshpot. It would be a noble pose. Maybe it would make the *Union-Leader.* Beyond that, in the dreamy distance, lay the *New York Times.* And think of the wire services, the talk shows.

12

D riving past the Queen of Softness's lunch counter about quarter to twelve that Tuesday night, I saw a light on in the back where she's got her little house: a soft red glow. I imagined her back there sewing sequins on a G-string, ruining her eyes for her art. Of course, I made sure that no other cars were parked nearby, some other mule kicking in my stall, but the Queen of Softness has a quality that I often lack: Fidelity. Sad to say, Diversity has been my motto, although as I move farther along in my sixties I find that the circumstances of my life increasingly force fidelity upon me.

It's pitiful. What in the past was a cheerful little invitation to the lady of your choice now gets called sexual harassment: not only do you get turned down, but you get punished for asking. But that's not quite true. It's not the young and handsome guys who get punished. So you are not just punished for asking, you are punished for being old and overweight. You get punished for being a geezer. And your guileless invitation to fun and frolic is not simply an insult to this lady's womanhood, it is an insult to her sense of herself as a beautiful woman, someone who thinks she deserves a lot more than an old fart in a Yugo. Although let me say when I borrowed that guy's Maserati for about fifteen minutes, I got quite a few inviting looks.

My windshield wipers were going: thwack, thwickthwick, THWACK. It wasn't quite syncopation; rather, it was what I had come to expect of the Yugo: a car that progressed through the world like a guy on crutches falling down a flight of stairs. I had to respect it. Like the car ought to have been dead but it kept going. Maybe it had heart, maybe it was simply stubborn. And the lights weren't as bright as I would like and the heater was busted and the tires wobbled. And the speed? Like sixty miles an hour made it sound like a grasshopper in love.

Up ahead were the taillights of Bobby's Honda Civic. It was about six years old like the Yugo, but it was faster. The taillights kept drawing away into little red pinpricks, then they would get brighter again when Bobby realized I wasn't keeping up. Once or twice I noticed headlights in my rearview mirror, some vehicle hanging way back. Probably a lonely farmer going home. It didn't occur to me to worry about it.

I crested the hill above Schuylerville, passing the apple orchards. All around here was where the Battle of Saratoga was once fought and there are little signs commemorating who did what. In fact, Schuylerville used to be called Saratoga but then got its name changed in honor of General Schuyler, who had made himself famous during the fighting. Like maybe he was in charge. The British troops grounded their arms at the surrender right by the post office. A long hill runs down, down, down to the main street because the town is set along the Hudson River. During racing season a bunch of yachts up from New York City are docked here. Like they are big in the way that King Kong was big. Why say "money talks" when it bellows, when it shouts from the rooftops? Does money need to be subtle? No way.

Bobby turned south on Route 4, for the little dogleg through the village. Except for streetlights, it seemed that all the lights were out in Schuylerville: lots of country folk dreaming the dreams of the just or the bored. I wondered how many were wearing Rosemary's sequined bikinis. We passed the big empty hotel, then turned east again on Route 29, passed the PO, then approached the bridge over the Hudson. Maybe some of these houses had little blue television lights, maybe the rain put people in a drowsy mood. Now and then my headlights caught the orange leaves of a maple that couldn't stand the suspense and decided to change color early. As I crossed over the bridge, I checked my rearview mirror again just to scare myself.

The problem with the vehicle that was hanging way back was that one of its headlights was slightly askew. Otherwise there would be no way to know that this particular vehicle had followed us all the way from Saratoga Springs. On the other hand, this was a well-traveled road with lots of little towns lying along it. The driver could be someone on a perfectly innocent errand: love or the promise of love, maybe a poor old janitor going home to the wife. Like there was nothing to say that I wasn't being paranoid.

The Yugo took the steep hill on the east side of the Hudson in third gear. There used to be a great restaurant back in the woods up on the bluff facing west. It was one of the best places in the world to see the sunset. Happy hour, stiff drinks, free eats, bright sunset—unfortunately it couldn't compete with TV and the place has been closed for quite a few years.

Up ahead on the flats Bobby was passing the fairgrounds of the Washington County Fair on his left. I had taken the Queen of Softness there in mid-August and won her a kewpie doll. We had eaten fried food and checked out the younger pigs and goats. We didn't take any of the rides this year, my stomach will no longer stand it. Some guy tried to guess Rosemary's age and missed by a decade. For this she won a Hershey bar which probably cost about a third what it cost to have this doofus guess her age in the first place.

As I passed the darkened fairground, I saw the vehicle with the crooked light just cresting the hill behind me. Maybe the person had gotten a little closer. On my right lay the Hand melon farm. That's a Dutch name rather than indicating the shape or consistency of the melons. Every morning at the track during racing season they serve Hand melons to the folks who have come for breakfast and to watch the horses working out. They have been serving Hand melons at the clubhouse for a lot longer than I have been on this planet. It's what some call a tradition and others call a monopoly.

I made the turn and descended through the sleepy hamlet of Middle Falls. Maybe a couple of geezers were still awake and looking at their wrinkled pusses in the mirror, wondering how much time they had left. Taxidermy is a big industry in Middle Falls, that and furniture stripping.

The biggest town along here before Cambridge is Greenwich—pronounced Green-witch—a town with pretty houses and pretty trees, but like most of these towns it has been busted by people doing their shopping in Saratoga. Bobby hung a left across from the library to stay on Route 29. As we drove out of town the Batten Kill was on my right. If you like trout, that's where you catch them. We were about fifteen miles from Saratoga. I kept one eye on the rearview mirror. Just before I made the first curve along the river, I saw the headlights. Whoever was behind us had made the turn and was picking up speed.

Bobby's plan was for me to talk to his cousin, Josh, and see Fleshpot, make sure he was all right and that he was the same horse that had been sold for half a million. Then I would rent a horse trailer in Cambridge first thing in the morning. Just what I was supposed to do with the horse wasn't entirely clear, but I knew a guy by the name of Carl Logan who had a horse farm just south of Schuylerville and I thought I could keep Fleshpot there for a few days, just long enough to let Bobby and Josh get away. Admittedly this was against the law and I didn't want to get Carl in trouble, but the law for me has always been a questionable enterprise. I'm here and it's there. Like the Ten Commandments, I respect them but I don't necessarily obey them. Also, it seemed obvious that once I showed up with the horse, the cops would have to forgive me.

For Bobby this business of swapping Fleshpot for a ringer was no more than a giggle. Pennyfeather had told them it would take ten days of their time. They flew into Kennedy from San Diego, then took the bus up to Saratoga. They had worked with horses in California. The ten grand they were picking up seemed like big money. Josh was thinking of going to community college, Bobby was thinking of scoring some coke and selling it at a profit. Five grand each for ten days of work seemed the ultimate good luck, although it hadn't worked out like that. Like the promise of all good luck there had been a catch.

"Every time we told Pennyfeather how we wanted to leave," Bobby had explained, "he'd say the cops were looking for us."

"What if you'd known that you were suspected of murder?" I asked.

"Shit, then we would of run for sure, horse or no horse."

The nice thing about being twenty is that you have a rudimentary sense of consequences. You understand that bad things happen, but you don't necessarily know why. Like lightning, right? Sometimes it hits here, sometimes there.

"After the horse sold for five hundred and thirty thousand," Bobby had told me, "I walked him back toward the barn. There were a lot of people hanging around and I wasn't sure the swap was going to work. Pennyfeather had said to pause right by the corner of Barn Four South, staying as close to the wall as possible. I didn't know what he was up to. Suddenly this other horse screams. I hang on to the colt just as this black horse comes rushing by, bucking and jumping. People scattered. They forgot all about me and my half-a-million-dollar animal. I led the colt through the gap in Barn Three. The ringer was in stall four of Barn Three West. Josh led her out. He looks like me and he was dressed like me. Like he was a ringer as well. Josh led out the ringer and I put the colt into stall number four and shut the door. The ringer went into Fleshpot's stall. You see, we been calling him Fleshpot as well. That night we slapped some color on him, changed his markings, grunged him up like a stable pony, then got him out first thing in the morning, mixed him in with the horses exercising over at the track, then got him out through the backstretch. Thursday the truck was supposed to show up and we would drive him to Miami, except that the truck never showed up. We been out there ever since. I tell you, it's been pretty dull and there's nothing good to eat."

It was on the stretch along the river between Center Falls and Battenville that the vehicle behind me started gaining fast. I wondered about the possibility of Pennyfeather following Bobby into Saratoga. How would he feel about Bobby parking outside my place? Then I had appeared and had started following Bobby back toward Sushan. How would Pennyfeather feel about this? No nice thoughts. No Christian charity. Like hadn't the guy already killed Paul Butterworth?

The rain had gotten worse and my windshield wipers were doing a terrible job: just smear, smear. The faster I went, the more the steering wheel shook from the tires being out of line. There wasn't any other traffic and the few houses which I passed were dark. By now it was past midnight.

When I saw the lights getting bigger in my mirror, I put the accelerator to the floor. But the Yugo wasn't built for speed. It wasn't built for comfort either, for that matter. It was built to be cheap transportation, one step up from the camel but half as dependable. Bobby's Honda Civic was about a quarter of a mile ahead of me. The skewed headlight of the vehicle behind me was the driver's headlight and it pointed up and off to the left. Both headlights seemed high and I thought that the vehicle might be a truck. You know how you can be frightened by little things? When the guy behind me flicked on his high beams, I felt absolutely terrified.

There was no way I could get any more speed out of the Yugo but I started flicking my lights so Bobby would know something bad was happening. Now the vehicle was coming up like I was standing still. Its high beams in my mirror made it hard to see and I shoved the mirror up out of the way. But the high beams made me think that the vehicle was one of those four-by-four pickups. I could even hear its rumble, like it was unhappy or mad. I thought how Charlie wouldn't let me carry a pistol. How I didn't even have a license for a pistol. I thought how sometime last year I had considered buying a shotgun and how I had decided against it. Who needs a shotgun? I had thought. I considered how I hadn't called the Queen of Softness that evening and told her I was crazy about her. And my new cellular phone? Tucked away in the belly drawer of my desk where it would be safe. Hey, I wouldn't want to bust it.

The trouble with my mirror pushed out of the way was that I couldn't see exactly where the vehicle behind me was located, even though the whole inside of the Yugo was flooded with light. I tilted the mirror and wished I hadn't. The truck's headlights were about two feet behind me. Two feet behind and two feet above. I was coming up fast on a little efficiency store that was closed for the night. It had a wooden sandwich board on the side of the road saying, "Nite-Crawlers 4 Sale." I swerved the wheel of the Yugo to the right, smashed the sign and slammed on the brakes all at the same time. The sign banged up over my car, hitting the pickup truck. The moment I slowed, the truck was already past me. I swerved back onto the highway again. One of my headlights was busted.

The truck took off fast: a Dodge Ram four-by-four with mud covering the rear license plate. The Honda had started to go faster as well but it was no good. I was falling behind but I still saw what happened clearly enough. It was like a badminton racket hitting a shuttlecock. The truck swerved out into the passing lane and just hung there for a minute. I couldn't think what it was waiting for until I saw both the truck and the Honda climbing the hill. There was just darkness off to my right, maybe fields, maybe nothing. The truck was hanging alongside the Honda and perhaps a little behind. The two sets of taillights made a blurry red line in the rain shooting up the hill ahead of me. At the top the truck swerved to the right. Abruptly, Bobby's pair of taillights disappeared like hocus pocus dominocus. There wasn't even any noise.

Then the truck crested the hill and for a moment it seemed that nothing was ahead of me, just rain and darkness. But as I got higher I saw a light jittering off the road to my right. At first I couldn't think what it was. Then I realized it was Bobby's Honda crashing down the hill toward the river. Just as that thought entered my mind, I saw a ball of fire, then, through my closed windows, came a dull explosion. I started pumping the brakes as I pulled off to the side of the road onto the gravel.

I didn't have a flashlight but the fire down the hill was burning fiercely and I could see my way. I hurried through a break in a wooden fence, then down through the wet grass, slipping and falling and getting up again. Even as a youngster I wasn't much of a runner. When you run at my age the knees make their little protests and the feet complain and the hips tell you how much they don't like it. Luckily, I was going downhill so I was falling as much as running.

The Honda had come to rest against a pile of rocks just up from the water. It was completely in flames although the rain was trying to do its work against them. I could see Bobby sitting in the front seat, just a black silhouette that wasn't moving. The front door was open and Bobby's hand was reaching out of the fire, but it wasn't moving either. It was just sticking out of the flames like a signpost. I could see the blue tattoo of the swallow on his forearm, then I watched it turn black. I stood and looked at it, feeling the heat from the fire on my face as the rain beat down upon me. Then Bobby's seat belt must have burned through, because he slowly fell forward onto the steering wheel and disappeared. Even if I could have grabbed that hand, there would have been no point in pulling him out. He was cinders already.

I turned and made my way back up the hill, still slipping and sliding. I realized I was cold and wet and that my body hurt. The flames from the burning car were dying down. As I thought about Bobby and his silly plans, I almost came to a stop. Then I started to run again. Josh was still off in the country with Flesh-pot. He would be expecting Bobby to come back. When the Dodge Ram four-by-four pulled up in front of the mill, who would Josh think it was? I hurried toward the Yugo parked on the side of the road, one smashed headlight, the other still burn-ing. The rain was hissing against the grass all around me. Then I heard something else: sirens.

I wasn't running exactly, but I was hurrying with a passion. By the time I reached the Yugo, I could see flashing lights com-ing from Greenwich. I figured some farmer had given the state cops a call. I yanked open the door, jumped inside, then couldn't find my keys. They weren't in any of my pockets. As the cop car approached, its headlights reflected off my key chain. The keys were in the ignition. I turned the key and the motor sputtered. Did I say before that the Yugo floods easily and has a hand choke? I shoved in the choke, took my foot off the gas and turned the key again. The engine sputtered and caught. I took off spitting gravel just as the cop car drew up behind me.

You know how these cop cars have speakers on the front so the cops can talk in a big Darth Vader voice? As I took off I heard this voice: "Stop immediately and put your hands on top of the steering wheel!"

I kept going. I figured the cop had a choice. To chase me or to investigate the Honda burning in the field. I guessed he would check out the Honda and I was right. In my mirror I saw two cops jump out of their car and head down the hill.

The road to Shushan was just up ahead, Route 61 in the middle of Battenville. I cut my lights, then made the right turn in the dark. Ahead of me more cop cars were approaching and I assumed the guy behind me had radioed his pals. I moved forward slowly and when the cops had passed, I flicked on my lights, or one single light, crossed the bridge over the Batten Kill and got moving again. Speaking about not knowing the consequences of your actions, I guess I was crazy to keep going, because I knew that Dodge Ram four-by-four had to be out there someplace and whoever was driving meant nothing nice.

But I thought how long it would take me to explain to the cops what was going on and how I didn't have much faith in their powers of understanding. Could I get it across to them in a half hour? And what else would have happened by that time? And unfortunately I kept seeing the photo of myself next to Fleshpot on the front page of the *Saratogian*. "Hero," it would say, or "Rescuer." Don't think I pat my own back. I've done lots of foolish things and maybe I'll do one or two others.

The old mill was right outside of Shushan, just off Route 64. The Batten Kill doubled around coming down out of the Green Mountains and the mill was perched right beside it. Bobby had shown me where it was on a map in case we got separated. I didn't need him in order to find it.

13

The first time I drove past the mill, I didn't see it because there weren't any lights on. Then I doubled back. It was a big old ramshackle building and maybe it just didn't have electricity, but then how had Bobby and Josh been playing their video games? The river was loud from the rain: telling stories as it made its way down to the Hudson. I turned off my lights and pulled up in front. Sometime in the past the building must have been white, now it was just weathered. I sat in the Yugo for a moment wondering why I wasn't home in bed or paying the Queen of Softness a nocturnal visit. But you know how something you have seen can keep repeating itself in memory like a little movie played across your eyes? I kept seeing the lights from Bobby's Honda bouncing down the hillside. And I could almost feel how scared he had been, hanging on to the wheel, being thrown all over, and then he had hit the rocks.

So tiptoeing away and going home to bed wasn't that simple. Josh had to be somewhere around here and Fleshpot as well. And even if I couldn't save them, at least I could warn them.

I opened the door of the Yugo and got out. The overhead

light has been broken for as long as I have had the car and so I didn't have to worry about that, but the door creaked. It was cool and my jacket was still wet from scrambling through the field earlier. My feet were wet and the ground was muddy. I made my way to the front of the building: slosh, slosh. The rain was letting up and there had to be a moon back behind the clouds because I could see shapes, like trees and bushes and the building itself. Even so, I thought of how Charlie Bradshaw always carried a flashlight in his car and how I didn't. The building was two stories and looked more like an old factory than a mill. Back sometime in the past Shushan had to have been a thriving metropolis, or ruralopolis.

The front door of the building was open and I wasn't sure how I felt about that. Was it a sign of welcome or a sign of trickery? I stepped inside. Bobby had said they had been keeping the horse in the back, so they could take him out behind the mill now and then to give him some fresh air. And once inside I could even smell the aroma of horse, which was, to some degree, reassuring. I considered calling out for Josh, then decided against it. Call it a sixth sense, or maybe it was just terror, but I didn't want to make any noise.

I was in a hallway and I made my way down it, keeping my right hand on the wall. There was some faint light coming in through the front door, but ahead of me everything was dark. Then the door slammed shut. You know how you can read the sentence "His heart was in his throat" and feel that it's an exaggeration? It's not. My heart was right up there and if my mouth hadn't been shut, my heart would have bounced out right onto the floor. I leaned against the wall, feeling the thumping in my chest and wondering if it was possible for my cholesterol level to explode. It's the wind, I kept telling myself, although I hadn't noticed the wind earlier.

I kept making my way down the hall. Every now and then I

would pass a door, sometimes open, sometimes closed. Maybe the horse smell was getting stronger. The building was dusty and there was a lot of crud on the floor: leaves and nails and paper. It was almost impossible to walk without making noise. The hallway abruptly ended at another hallway which ran perpendicular to it. I say abruptly because I ran into the wall, bumping my forehead and banging my nose. Why is it that whenever you bang your nose, you feel silly? I stopped and listened. I thought I could hear movement, but it might have been rats. It occurred to me that it would be a mistake to surprise Josh. I mean, if I was scared, he had to be scared too.

"Hey, Josh!" I called. "Josh, it's Vic Plotz!"

No answer.

"Josh, you in here?"

Nothing.

But then, unfortunately, I heard a board creak. And I might have thought that was the wind as well, if that same board hadn't made the same exact creak when I had stepped on it about three minutes earlier. I do not know if you have had the experience of becoming aware that someone is following you through the dark, but it is not pleasant. I mean, the first thing you realize is that the person behind you means nothing nice. No flowers, no kisses, no chocolates. He or she is creeping along in the dark as quietly as possible because he or she means to do something nasty. It's sad, but it's true.

I turned right in the hallway and tried to move forward quickly. By now it was so dark that I couldn't even see my hand in front of my face. I don't know what was on the floor: pieces of wood, chunks of plaster, more papers, now and then a tin can or a bottle. I seemed to hit them all and every time I made a noise, I told myself to keep quiet. I stayed by the wall. Apart from kicking the stuff on the floor, maybe my breathing was making a lot of noise and maybe my heart was pounding loudly. I kept my right hand against the wall and when I came to an open space, I almost fell. It was a flight of stairs. I went up them, again keeping my weight to the side so the steps wouldn't creak. Hey, they creaked no matter what I did. I reached the top and found myself in a large room. On the other side, about twenty feet away, I could make out the outline of a window. I stood at the top of the stairs and tried to breathe as quietly as possible. Then I heard a noise beneath me. It was somebody beginning to climb the stairs, someone who was trying to move quietly, someone up to no good.

I suppose I should have stayed at the top of the stairs and whacked whoever was sneaking along. That's what James Bond would have done. Maybe that is even what Charlie Bradshaw would have done. But when you are sixty or thereabouts, your body has another agenda: flight. There was a draft coming through the window. As I got closer to it, I could see that it was broken. Maybe I was thinking of jumping, but when I looked out and saw my Yugo down below, I got cold feet. It was a long way. Earlier that summer I had gotten a flier from the YMCA which had printed across it in big black letters: "Out of Shape?" That was as far as I read before I junked it. Now, for some reason, it came back to me, like the letters were embossed across the darkness. *"Out of Shape?"* But even if I had been in great shape, I wouldn't have wanted to jump out that window.

Then I saw someone down by my car, or rather I saw a thin figure. I called out, "Josh, hey, Josh, it's Vic Plotz!" The figure ducked back into the shadows. This was disheartening. It meant there were two people who were trying to keep themselves hidden from me. And as I thought that, I heard the floor creak. I spun around but it was too late. Something whacked me on the side of the head. Or maybe I just felt the pain, like my whole head had popped open. There were even bright lights, although nobody was taking my picture. No snapshots for posterity. And then I saw nothing at all.

. . .

When I came to, there was light all around me: orange and red and yellow. Also I was being severely jostled. Also I was upside down. There's a long distance between unconsciousness and waking, and there are a lot of stops along the way. Like it's the journey from ignorance to knowledge and it has to be done slowly. My head hurt. My guts hurt and were being bounced in an unpleasant way. There was smoke and heat and a snapping and crackling. Flames were swinging back and forth across my vision.

Then enlightenment struck. A fireman's carry, that's what was going on. I was the victim of a fireman's carry and the guy who was the perpetrator was bouncing down a flight of stairs.

"Hey!" I said.

"Keep still!" said the guy. It wasn't a fireman. It was someone who smelled of horse, although all I could see from my angle was a black nylon jacket and a pair of Levi's.

"Put me down!" I said.

We reached the bottom of the stairs and the guy dumped me onto my feet. I promptly collapsed. I was dizzy. Even though I wasn't moving, everything was moving around me. I looked up and saw Josh Flynn standing above me. His face was moving in a circle, but when I concentrated I saw that he looked impatient.

"The building's on fire," he said. "If we stay here, we'll get cooked."

He pulled me to my feet. I shut my eyes for a moment and the floor settled down, no more spinning. I opened them again and saw Josh staring at me. Then he grabbed my arm and half pulled and half carried me down the hall. The air was full of smoke and I kept coughing. There were flames behind us and I could see flames through cracks in the ceiling. Some pieces of paper on the floor were burning. My head still hurt and I had to work hard to put one foot in front of the other. But a burning building is a powerful motivator. So is a strong guy dragging on your arm. I saw a door ahead of us. It was closed but we lurched toward it. Josh kicked it open and a cool breeze hit my face. We stumbled outside. Josh let go of my arm. I took a few steps, then splashed down in the mud. He dragged me up again and we took a few more steps. Then I sat down again.

"Let me get my breath," I said. The mud felt nice and cool on my backside. I pressed a handful against my head where it hurt. Maybe it helped. At least it was a distraction. The whole upstairs of the mill was on fire and part of the downstairs as well. We were behind the building right by the river. The fire was hot on my face. Josh helped me to my feet again.

"Where's Bobby?" he said. "Did you see him?"

"He's dead," I told him.

Josh grabbed my jacket. "What the fuck happened?"

"Somebody ran him off the road, someone in a Dodge Ram. He crashed. I'm sorry. I came out here to tell you. Where's the horse?"

Josh put his hands to his head. "Jesus, oh Jesus."

He was younger than Bobby, about eighteen, and right now he looked around fifteen. His black hair was wet and smeared over his forehead. There was mud on his hands, which he kept pressed to his face.

I took his arm. "We've got to get out of here. Where's the horse?"

"I got him tied to a tree out in the woods."

"Did you start the fire?"

"No, I don't know who did."

I thought about crowding a horse into the backseat of my Yugo. Even if I cut him up in little pieces, he wouldn't fit. I looked at Josh, who stood there shaking his head and weeping. His face was smeared with muddy fingerprints. With every second the fire was getting worse. The flames had broken through the roof and were leaping into the sky. The air around us was burning up. There was a crash as something fell, a mass of sparks rose up into the dark. I thought of the Yugo parked around the front of the building.

"I got to move my car," I said.

I tried to run, but I was still too dizzy. Maybe I staggered. The ground was muddy and grabbed at my feet. Each window of the old mill was bright with flames. It was strange being sopping wet and burning up at the same time. My clothes were steaming. I figured that the fire could be seen for miles. Right now somebody was calling the fire department, or what passed for a fire department in Shushan, volunteers most likely.

I rounded the front of the building and there was my Yugo, burning. A section of wall had fallen on top of it and the seats were on fire and the paint was bubbling on the hood and roof. There was no way I could move it and at any moment the gas tank would go up. It looked like I had just sold it to the insurance company, except, of course, it hadn't been insured.

Then, as I stood there, I realized that someone was lying next to the car, maybe two or three feet from the burning section of wall. I ran toward him. I didn't think I would make it because the heat was burning my face, and I kept thinking about my gas tank and how I had filled it just that evening. It was a guy in a dark sweatshirt and sweatpants and he was lying on his belly. I grabbed one of his feet and began to pull. He didn't slide easy and I don't think I was going anyplace. But then Josh grabbed the other foot. The guy had nice new running shoes but I didn't think he had been a jogger. We both pulled like crazy back toward the road and the river. Maybe we got about twenty feet when the gas tank blew.

I got knocked back a couple of yards and fell back into the mud. I lay there, tucked up and covering my head. There was a lot of debris clattering around me. Like it was raining Yugo. I suppose I was lucky not to be killed by the shrapnel: get a rear fender through my gut. All that clunked me was one of my windshield wipers which came down and hit my hand. I lay there and considered the unhappiness of my body. Every pore was making its little howl. The bones hurt, the muscles hurt. I began to think of retirement, the quiet life. Couldn't I go someplace quiet and learn to knit, sell sweaters at Saturday market days? Maybe keep a couple of hens?

But Josh was tugging at me again. "You all right?"

He helped me to my feet, that is, he dragged me up. I wobbled a little. There was blood on Josh's face.

"You're cut," I said.

He wiped a hand across his face, smearing the blood into the dirt. "It's nothing."

I turned back to the third of our party, who was still lying facedown in the mud. I knelt and turned him over. It was Jerry Pennyfeather and he looked at me with the dull sort of look that indicates a lack of thought processes. Like he was no longer among the living. His dark bangs were all muddy and he had stopped resembling Moe in the Three Stooges. A corpse doesn't look like anything but a corpse.

"It's Pennyfeather," I said. "He's dead."

"Was it the fire?" Josh was standing back, not wanting to look. I liked that he was squeamish. It made me feel not so bad about my own squeamishness.

"Not unless the fire shot him right between the eyes," I said. "Did you shoot him, by the way?"

"No, sir. I don't even have a gun."

"Then there's somebody else." There was nothing pleasant about that thought. I wondered who had clunked me on the head. And I wondered where that other person was right at that moment.

"We got to get out of here," said Josh.

He set off down the road and I followed him. "We have to get the horse," I said.

"He's tied up along here."

We had gone about thirty feet when I saw the flicker of a red light. It was a reflector lit up by the flames of the burning mill. I pushed toward it through the bushes. It was the Dodge Ram four-by-four which had been pulled off the road.

"That's Jerry's truck," said Josh.

"That's the truck that shoved your cousin off the highway," I told him. I ran to the cab and opened the door. The keys were missing. I figured they were in Jerry's pocket.

"How far is Fleshpot?" I asked.

"He's up the road a little bit."

"Go get him and bring him back. I'll see if Jerry's got the keys." I turned and ran back toward the fire. No, not ran. I can't run anymore, remember? I hurried.

I guess undertakers and coppers do it all the time, but I find something nasty about going through a dead man's pockets. I kept imagining that Jerry would grab my wrist. He was wet from the rain and the pockets of his sweatpants were clammy. Not only were they clammy, they were also empty. Then I saw that Jerry was wearing one of those kangaroo pouches around his waist. I yanked off the whole thing and unzipped it. The keys were inside. I kept the pouch and hurried back to the truck.

The nice thing about the Dodge Ram was that it started right away. My Mercedes used to do that. The Yugo would sometimes start and sometimes wouldn't start—it depended on the condition of its Serbian soul. I have to say I felt a touch of guilty pleasure at the thought of the Yugo being blown to smithereens, gone to that great Kosovo in the sky. I put the truck in reverse and slowly backed up to the road. Then I turned away from the mill. In the headlights I could see Josh coming down the road with a big chestnut colt: Fleshpot. He kept tossing his head, not liking the flames one bit. Had the circumstances been different I would have leapt from the truck and embraced him.

We still had a big problem, which was how could we get

Fleshpot into the back of the pickup and, once he was there, how could we make him stay put? You want to know why horse vans are covered? So the horses can't see what is going on. It's the old horse motto again: Keep them relaxed.

Josh opened the back gate and I backed the truck around to the side of the road where there was a ditch and a little rise. Even so, it took both of us to get Fleshpot into the truck. Josh blind-folded him and led him forward. I lifted his front left leg onto the bed of the truck. Then Josh pulled and I pushed. He wasn't a bad horse, just scared. Once he was inside, I slammed the back gate. The four-by-four didn't have a full-sized bed and Josh and the horse looked crammed in. The floor was metal, of course, and Fleshpot kept slipping.

"Can't you make him lie down?" I said.

"Jesus, he's not a dog."

"Do tell," I said.

I got back in the cab. "You got to hang on to him."

There were sirens again. It seemed that I couldn't go anyplace that night without sirens. I turned up the road away from the mill, then turned right on Route 64. The sirens got louder. Maybe I was going about ten miles an hour, maybe less, because if Fleshpot had wanted to, he could have hopped out of the back of the pickup with no trouble, even though Josh was hanging on to him.

There were sirens and flashing lights ahead of me. Before I could decide to stop, an old fire truck went shooting past. There was a whinny and lots of clomping from Fleshpot, but he stayed in the truck. In the next two or three miles about six cars with flashing blue lights went roaring past, all of them volunteer fire-men. As each shot past I could see the driver staring up at the four-by-four in surprise. Fleshpot's head was sticking up over the cab like the prow of a ship.

14

Even though the Queen of Softness likes her late-night visits, I thought I might be pushing it. First of all it took a long time to get over to her place, partly because I couldn't take the main roads and partly because I didn't want to dump Fleshpot out into the gravel. It had started raining again and the bed of the truck was slippery. Even Josh had trouble keeping his balance. By the time I got through Schuylerville and over toward Saratoga, it was almost four in the morning. Rosemary's lunch counter opens at six for breakfast so I figured she would be getting up soon. In any case, her place was the nearest place I could think of and I had to get Fleshpot hidden.

When Bobby had first told me about Pennyfeather earlier in the evening, I had felt a sense of closure. Like he was the guy who had stolen the horse. The mystery was over. And even though I hadn't been positive that Pennyfeather had been driving the four-by-four that ran Bobby off the road, I had been pretty sure it was him. And the guy following me through the dark in the mill, that had to be Pennyfeather too. He had clunked me with something and that had been that. But just before he clunked me, I had seen someone outside, someone who had been neither Josh nor Pennyfeather. In fact, that someone had presumably shot Pennyfeather, because Pennyfeather himself hadn't had a gun. Or at least there hadn't been one on his body and there hadn't been one in his little kangaroo pouch. So the mystery which had been neatly closed was opened again. Who shot Pennyfeather?

I don't suppose it really put a crimp in my relationship with Rosemary that I showed up at her place at four-thirty in the morning with a wanted felon and a stolen horse, but it surprised her. Josh was covered with mud and he had blood on his face. I don't know what made me think I looked any better. And we were wet, even the horse. I pulled the four-by-four behind Rosemary's bungalow so that it couldn't be seen from the road. She doesn't have a garage, but she has a small shed where she keeps her tractor mower and garden stuff. There was a little hill back there and I put the four-by-four next to it so that Fleshpot could climb out fairly easily. The trouble is that he didn't want to. First he didn't want to get into the truck and then he didn't want to get out. Fickle. I pushed him backward and Josh set one of his back feet on the ground. During all this, which included loudly whispered directions and encouragements to the horse, the lights came on in Rosemary's bungalow, one by one. Then, would you believe it, once we get Fleshpot down on the solid ground and take off his blindfold, he leans forward and nips my backside so I yell.

Rosemary called out, "Victor, is that you?"

"Goldarn horse! Don't you know I saved you from an early grave?"

"Victor, it's raining," called Rosemary.

I began to say something rude but stopped myself. Taking Fleshpot's bridle, I led him over to Rosemary, who was standing in her back door wearing her scarlet silk robe and holding a .22 rifle.

"I was going to shoot until I heard you cry out," she said. "Why do you have a horse?"

"This is Fleshpot," I said. It occurred to me that by nipping my backside Fleshpot had saved my life. Josh had gotten back in the four-by-four and driven it up behind the bungalow. Now he got out and joined me.

Rosemary stared at us. Her platinum-blond hair was a little mussed but she looked kindly. "You both have blood on your faces," she said.

"We've been having our troubles," I said.

"You better come inside," said Rosemary.

Sad to say, Fleshpot had to stay out in the wet weather. Rosemary's ceilings were low and the horse would have dented the kitchen linoleum, or worse. But Josh tethered him under the overhang so he could stay out of the rain if he wanted to. I guess it is obvious to say that a horse is big, but when you are trying to heave one around they seem enormous.

Once we were inside, Rosemary grew even more concerned about the blood on our faces. Mine was from where I had been bashed on the head. Josh's cheek had been slashed by a piece of the exploding Yugo. And, as I say, we were covered with mud. Rosemary shoved us toward the bathroom and began tending us. When Josh tried to protest, Rosemary simply pushed him.

A half hour later all three of us were sitting in her kitchen. Josh and I were wearing silk kimonos: Josh's was pink, mine was purple. Our clothes were in the washing machine, which was churning happily. We were drinking coffee and I had added a dollop of brandy to mine. It was still raining but the sky was getting a little lighter to the east.

I was telling them about Bobby's visit and then what had happened when we had driven out to Shushan. I described how the Dodge Ram had knocked Bobby's Honda off the road. As I spoke the words, I could see the images before me, the big four-by-four swerving to the right and shoving the Honda into the dark. Rosemary looked serious. Josh was weeping and wiping his eyes on the back of his hand. Then I told about how I had driven on to the mill and all that happened there. Rosemary had cleaned the wound on my head, trimmed away the hair and put on a bandage. Even so, it still hurt. Josh had several small bandages on the cuts on his face. The only good thing to tell was that I no longer had the Yugo. It had become a car angel.

Josh, it turned out, knew even less than Bobby about what had happened at the yearling sales. It had been Bobby who dealt with Pennyfeather and had convinced Josh to come east. Josh hadn't even realized that they had come to steal a horse until they had been in Saratoga a week. He had never been east before and it was a treat. He especially liked New York City. But then Bobby had told him they were in the business of stealing a horse. I could almost guess the day when Josh learned the ugly news: say that time between when he had been friendly and when he had been nervous. He said Pennyfeather had come out to the mill several times to bring supplies, but he had always talked to Bobby by himself. Josh had no idea who the third person could have been. No other names had been mentioned. I asked if it could be Henry O'Leary, but Josh just shrugged.

"When Bobby told me we had to kill the horse," Josh said, "I didn't want to have anything to do with it. I told him I'd leave. He didn't want to kill the horse either. I mean, the horse trusted us. There were some old apple trees behind the mill and we gave him apples. I don't know how we were supposed to kill him. We didn't even have a gun. So I convinced Bobby to go talk to you. I don't know, if we had killed the horse, at least Bobby would still be alive. Don't you think?"

There was nothing I could say to that. It was one of those

things that might be true but there was nothing you could do about it. Looking at Josh, I kept seeing his cousin Bobby because they looked so much alike: the same long black hair that kept falling over their eyes, the same straight nose and narrow face, the same height and thin shape. The same little gold stud in their left earlobes. Ringer horses, ringer cousins. And was there a ringer killer as well? But I was hardly thinking clearly. I was dead tired and Josh was tired too. And my body hurt, all my pores joined together into a chorus of woe. I kept trying to think what we could do with the horse, but nothing came to mind. It was past five-thirty and Rosemary had to open the lunch counter.

"Get some sleep," she said, "and I'll try to find out what the police are up to." She had a police radio in the restaurant and liked to listen to state cop chat.

"Don't let anyone see the horse," I said.

Josh got the couch and I got the water bed. I rarely spent the night at Rosemary's, since long visits make a woman feel proprietorial, especially if you wake up in her bed in the morning. The water bed for me was where the Queen of Softness and I navigated our passion, but passion that morning was not a hot item on my emotional agenda. I sloshed back and forth under the fake-leopard-skin coverlet and stared at the animal paintings on black velvet. There was a stag on a mountaintop, listening to something far away. I was just wondering what he was listening to when I fell asleep.

I woke up to find somebody shaking my arm. It was Rosemary. She looked frightened.

"Victor, you've got to leave. The police are searching for you all over. You're wanted for murder, arson, all kinds of things. It's been on the radio for the past twenty minutes. They're bound to come here. Get up." Rosemary had on the red jumpsuit with pearl buttons that she likes to wear in the restaurant.

"What time is it?" I sat up in bed, bouncing slightly as the water sloshed.

"Ten-thirty. I've got your clothes ready."

"Where's Josh?"

"I just woke him."

I got dressed as Rosemary went off to make us sandwiches and prepare a thermos of coffee. The trouble was that we couldn't just drive around with a horse in the back of a pickup truck. Like maybe we could avoid the cops for about five minutes. Once I was dressed, I called Charlie's home number. It rang and rang. He hates answering machines. Then I called his office. The phone rang and rang there as well. Then I called Janey Burris. Again there was no answer. I thought of other people I could call. That meant, who else would face an accessory charge on my account? I began to regret not spending my mature years becoming Mr. Popularity. The news that Vic Plotz was being hunted by the police would be happy news for lots of folks. I could almost hear the chuckles from where I sat.

In five more minutes we were ready to go. All we could do was to hide out until it got dark. Along Route 29 between Saratoga and Schuylerville there are sections of old Route 29 which are mostly just open places in the woods with some remnants of pavement, although in a couple of places there are houses along them as if the old part of the road was a private driveway. One of these disused sections was about a mile away. The plan was for me to drive there and Josh would lead Fleshpot through the woods. It was still raining: September 23rd, the autumn equinox. And could winter be far behind? I gave Rosemary a kiss on the cheek and headed for the truck, carrying the bag with the sandwiches and thermos of coffee. Before I left, however, I checked Rosemary's shed and took the ramp that she used to drive her tractor mower up into a truck bed. I figured Fleshpot could climb it as well.

I had no trouble driving over to the unused section of road. I put the truck in four-wheel drive, then plowed through the brush. Once I was in about fifty yards, I went back, pulled up some bushes and covered the entrance where the truck had pressed down the grass. By the time I got back to the four-by-four, I heard a noise coming through the trees and shortly Josh showed up with Fleshpot. I must say that apart from his unfortunate interest in people's backsides, Fleshpot was an affable and well-behaved animal. Here we had been dragging him all over and he was without complaint. Josh had brought a couple of apples and fed them to the horse, who chomped them noisily. Then Josh and I got in the cab. We were wet again. I started the truck to get the heater going, then I poured us some coffee.

"So what's the plan?" asked Josh.

"We'll wait until it's dark, then I'll call my friend Charlie Bradshaw." In fact, I would have driven over to his cottage on the lake, but he had nowhere to hide the horse and nowhere to hide the Dodge Ram four-by-four. And of course with the coppers looking for us, we might not have made it that far. A couple of times I considered giving myself up to the police, but there was no way that I could prove there was some third person out at the mill. Without that third person, I became the main suspect.

Also, there was still the problem of Paul Butterworth's murder. Pennyfeather might have been responsible for that. After all, he liked to hit people on the head. But Josh could easily be charged for it and I could be charged for it as well. In fact, there was no reason for the police to think that Pennyfeather was responsible for anything. Given these possibilities, it seemed unlikely that I would be released on bail. Probably I would have to sit in jail until the trial, and then who knew what would happen? These were not happy thoughts.

"What can your friend Bradshaw do?" asked Josh. He was eating a salami sandwich and had his mouth full.

I thought about that. "Maybe he can help find who killed Pennyfeather. Are you sure he never mentioned any names?"

"No, I hardly saw him."

"And your cousin?"

"He said Pennyfeather was running it."

"And you saw nobody else last night?"

"Nobody. Bobby said to wait in the woods if Pennyfeather showed up. He got there and then you showed up. A little after that the fire started."

"And did you hear a gunshot?"

"I don't know. I mean, the fire was making a lot of noise."

I kept kicking something on the floor. I shoved it to one side, then looked to see what it was. It was the pouch I had taken off Pennyfeather's corpse. I unzipped it, then took out a wallet. License, credit cards, agent's license, some business cards. He had a bunch of receipts and nearly five hundred smackers in cash. I divided the money into two equal portions and gave one pile to Josh.

"Here's your share," I said.

Josh looked at it doubtfully. "Isn't that stealing?"

"You think Pennyfeather's going to complain?"

Josh stuck the money in an inside pocket of his black nylon jacket. If we got separated, then at least he would have money to get away. I dug into the pouch again. Cigarettes, matches, a pen, a little notebook and an address book. As I was digging through this stuff, Josh got comfortable, watched me for a while, then went to sleep. Fleshpot was tied to the truck with a rope I had taken from Rosemary's shed. Through my window I could barely see the highway through the trees. Now and then a car passed.

The notebook had shopping lists, a few telephone numbers next to some initials, a few reminders ("Pick up shirts"), some doodles (a man smoking a cigar, a couple of stars and triangles) and a series of numbers which made no sense to me but might have been picks for different races. A couple of pages had columns of numbers which were then added up with a dollar sign. I put away the notebook and checked the address book. It had about a hundred names, although in many cases there were just initials. I saw Henry O'Leary's name and number, the Fasig-Tipton numbers in Saratoga and in Lexington, the number of Henrietta Farms. I felt certain that somewhere in the notebook or the address book was the information as to who had shot Pennyfeather, but I didn't know how to find it or how to look for it. I took the receipts out of the wallet again and began making a list of them on one of the back pages of the notebook. Shopping receipts from the Grand Union, credit card receipt from Trustworthy Hardware, dinner receipt from the Firehouse Restaurant in Saratoga, credit card receipt for gasoline from the Mobil station in Ballston Spa, several other restaurant receipts. The only other thing in the wallet was a racing ticket from the fifth race on August 26th at Saratoga: the number four horse to win. I wondered why Pennyfeather hadn't thrown it away. I thought about these problems for a while, all the why and wherefores, as I grew drowsier and drowsier, then I went to sleep as well.

It rained all day and the pattering sound on the roof of the truck had a melancholy quality. The wind whipped the branches around us. I felt sorry for Fleshpot getting soaked and I told myself that wherever I took him, it would have to be someplace inside. Josh slept for most of the day. Like a dog or cat he was able to turn himself off when nothing was happening. I kept remembering being pursued through the old mill and the fire. I kept seeing Bobby's car careening down the hill out of control and Pennyfeather lying on the ground with a bullet hole in his forehead. It was thoughts like this that made me wonder why I didn't go to Chicago and move in with my son, Matthew, and his wife and three kids, my grandkids. They got a nice brick house in Evanston. Matthew's in charge of his own lab in some Chicago hospital, a big one. What the hell, three days of that and I would probably die in my sleep. One more desperate oldster killed by boredom.

By six-thirty it was dark enough. I woke up Josh, we ate another salami sandwich, then I slowly drove back to the highway as he walked behind with Fleshpot. The horse didn't much like the tractor mower ramp but we got him up it. Twice he tried to nip my backside but I was too quick for him. Fleshpot's head stuck up over the cab. He was looking around, sort of curious. He had burrs in his tail and mane, mud on his legs. Josh got back there with him to try to hold him down, although if Fleshpot felt like it, he could hop out perfectly easily. I got off Route 29 onto Burgoyne Road going over toward Lake Saratoga. Maybe we passed three cars and I winced every time. It occurred to me that we could tie some branches to Fleshpot's head so it would look like we were transporting a tree.

I skirted the lake, taking back roads, working my way around the outskirts of Saratoga. A Chevy passed us with a couple of teenagers hanging out the window, pointing at Fleshpot. I smiled and waved at the little fuckers. I got back by the harness track, crossed Broadway over by the Spa City Diner, then began working my way through the side streets on the west side of town. Like there was almost nobody around, but almost nobody is not the same as nobody. Little kids waved to us. A guy walking his dog stopped and stared. A boy on a bike chased us for two blocks, then gave up.

There was an alley running behind Janey Burris's house over by the train station. She's got a big three-story Victorian house, pretty dilapidated and in need of paint. The backyard has some big maples. I remembered that the house had a coal cellar with an outside entrance. I was glad about that. It meant that I wouldn't have to lead Fleshpot through the kitchen.

15

Even though I had known Janey for quite a few years, you can never be sure when you might be stepping over the limit, crossing the line which you should never cross. I thought about that as I stood on her back stoop knocking on her door and letting the rain beat down upon my head. One of her daughters came to the door, then another, then the third, then they were replaced by Janey, who looked out with her hand at her forehead, shielding her eyes from the kitchen light. When she recognized me, she opened her eyes wide and pulled open the door.

"Victor, what are you doing at the back door in the rain?"

"Well," I said, "I brought a friend."

Janey gave me a quizzical look. She's got short black hair that she seems to cut with nail scissors so every strand points in a different direction. She was wearing her white nurse's uniform and white nurse's shoes.

"But you still could have come to the front door," she said.

"Well," I said, "I brought two friends. One of them's a horse."

Janey gave me the sort of look that a person gives you when they think you are making a joke but they just haven't gotten it yet: friendly, yet suspicious. I gave a wave of my hand to Josh, who was waiting under one of the trees with Fleshpot. He came forward, leading the horse with a rope. Janey saw Josh first and smiled, a welcoming cheerful smile, the smile of a person who doesn't mind being disturbed at eight o'clock in the evening by a stranger. Then she caught a glimpse of Fleshpot. Her smile didn't so much disappear as slide down her face.

"A horse," she said.

Immediately, Janey's three daughters were pushing around her. "A horse!" they echoed.

"Oh, Ma, can we keep him?" asked the youngest, who was about twelve.

I have never understood this passion that exists in the hearts of young girls for the equine beast. Like it's the book that Freud never got around to writing. It's kinky and not kinky all at once. These girls had known me for seven or eight years and tolerated me as a friend of Charlie's. Now I was Donald Trump and Santa Claus rolled into one.

"That's *your* horse, Mr. Plotz?" asked Emma, who was sixteen and well on her way to womanhood.

"Call me Vic," I said.

We opened up the outside door and led Fleshpot down into the cellar. He didn't like it much but at least he didn't bump his head. The first thing he did when he got into the cellar was to take a dump.

"Oh, look," said the girls. They could not have been happier.

We got Fleshpot into a room about the size of a stall where coal used to be stored. All three girls had run outside to gather handfuls of grass in the rain. Janey was looking rather dazed. Josh had gone out to get some grass as well. I mean, I thought of Janey's girls as babies, but Josh was just two years older than

Emma. Fleshpot made a loud whinny and clomped his foot down on the concrete.

"I think you have surpassed yourself this time, Victor," said Janey. I guess she was bemused. At least she wasn't angry.

"I got serious problems," I said.

"Somehow I already guessed that."

Once we got Fleshpot settled, Josh went off to get rid of the Dodge Ram, which, most likely, about ten thousand cops were looking for. I liked Josh. He had a sense of humor. He parked the Dodge right behind police headquarters, then he hiked back across town.

I had to tell the girls about Fleshpot. "One, he bites. Two, he's worth half a million dollars. Three, he's stolen." That seemed to cover it well enough. "Do not tell anybody that he is here, otherwise we all go to jail."

"Would that mean we'd lose the horse?" asked the youngest daughter.

"You bet," I said.

Janey had given me a big glass of Jim Beam green and stood over by the cellar stairs with her hand covering her eyes. I couldn't tell exactly what she was thinking, other than surprise. Fleshpot was munching grass.

"We won't tell anyone," said Emma.

The girls had found brushes and were getting the burrs out of Fleshpot's tail and mane. These were not horse brushes but colorful plastic brushes meant for little girls' hair. I don't know, there is something scary about a twelve-year-old, a fourteen-year-old and a sixteen-year-old with a passionate sense of mission. It makes you realize how that kook Joan of Arc got as far as she did. At least Fleshpot seemed happy-ish. Janey and I went back upstairs to her kitchen.

"How long do you plan to keep him here?" asked Janey, as if trying to make light conversation.

"Until we find out who killed Pennyfeather," I said. I began to tell her about it, but was interrupted by the ringing of her front doorbell. Janey went to see who it was.

It was Charlie. He began jabbering the moment he entered the hall. I stood by the kitchen door and he didn't see me.

"I just got back from Albany," he said. "There are roadblocks all over. Every policeman in the county is looking for Victor. My buddy." Charlie's hair was standing up straight. There were drops of water on his tan raincoat. "He's wanted for three different murders. He's wanted for arson. He's wanted for horse theft. He's wanted for car theft. And he's wanted for half a dozen lesser charges, any of which could put him away for a long time. I think the police have orders to shoot on sight. He's a dead man."

I stepped into the hall. "Surprise!" I said. At that moment a noisy whinny rose dramatically from the basement.

The word "nonplus" has a long and interesting history. It means the state at which no more can be said or done, as in to be at a nonplus. *Non* (or *ne*) *plus ultra,* meaning "not more beyond," was inscribed on the Pillars of Hercules, the mountains of Gibraltar and Abyla at the mouth of the Mediterranean, warning sailors not to enter the Atlantic, which was full of dangers. But when Charles V became emperor of Spain, which at that time included a large chunk of America, he made *Plus Ultra* the Spanish royal motto, meaning that even if other countries couldn't go further, Spain could and did and would. Charlie, as he stood in Janey's doorway, was in that state in which no more can be said or done. He was flummoxed.

"Jesus, Victor!"

"Aren't you going to say hello?"

"Oh, Victor, you're in trouble."

"It looks like Christmas in jail," I said.

"And all the Christmases to come," added Charlie.

But shortly we were in Janey's kitchen sipping whiskey,

which is a great reviver. After a few minutes Josh showed up and Charlie said "Jesus!" a few more times. Especially when he heard where Josh had parked the Dodge Ram. You know, considering how fond Charlie is of Jesse James and Billy the Kid and John Dillinger, you would think he would show more sympathy for a good buddy who accidentally found himself on the wrong side of the law, but he just kept scratching his head and riling his hair.

"So what happened, Victor?" he asked.

I explained how Bobby, who we used to know as Harry Macklin, had shown up at my apartment the previous night. It was a long story and it included a lot of adventures. The fire, the murder, the destruction of the Yugo. I showed the bandage on my head. I explained how we had driven to Rosemary's. A little earlier I had called her from Janey's and she had said that the cops had been out there five times. We didn't talk long. I mean, her phone might have been bugged. I told Charlie how we had driven into Saratoga with the horse in the back of the Dodge Ram and how kids had followed on their bikes. I ended with, "So you want to see Fleshpot? He's right downstairs."

We trooped down to the basement. Fleshpot was munching apples as the girls continued to brush him. They had braided his tail and made little braids in his mane into which they had woven pink, blue and yellow ribbons. Actually, I was surprised that Fleshpot wasn't wearing lipstick.

"Good grief," said Charlie.

"Can't we keep him, Ma?" asked the twelve-year-old again.

"You know," said Charlie, "every single one of us could go to jail." He said this as he might have said that the world was round or that two plus two made four.

We trooped back upstairs and Charlie poured himself some more whiskey, a big glass. He kept shaking his head and looking at the floor. Janey watched him.

"How long do you plan to keep that horse hidden in the basement?" asked Charlie.

"Until we catch whoever killed Pennyfeather."

"We?"

"You and me."

"And how long do you think it's going to remain a secret that Janey's got a horse in her basement?"

"You tell me."

"About until tomorrow morning when her daughters hit the streets."

"Oh, no," said Janey, "they can do better than that."

"Tomorrow afternoon then," said Charlie.

We continued this chitchat for a while as Charlie exercised his sense of humor. It's a weak and puny thing and he has to regularly take it out for a walk. But I could see that all this talk about jail was frightening Josh, and Janey didn't like it much either. It occurred to me that putting me and Charlie in jail might be the capstone of Peterson's career. His last act as Commissioner of Public Safety could be to send us away for life. Oh, happy day.

Once Charlie had calmed down, I took out Pennyfeather's kangaroo pouch and emptied its contents on the kitchen table. "It's not as if we don't have clues," I said. "The name of the killer has got to be in here someplace."

Charlie leafed through the notebook, then the address book. "That's like saying that the killer's name has got to be in the phone book. There're hundreds of names here."

"But we can eliminate a bunch and then you can start working on them."

Charlie picked up the ticket from the fifth race on August 26th at Saratoga. "What's this?" he asked.

"He didn't throw it away or maybe it's a winner," I said. "Pennyfeather didn't confide in me."

Janey reached for the cigarettes. "At least he won't be needing these anymore," she said.

Charlie looked into the wallet. "And he didn't have any money?"

"Credit cards, Charlie," I said. "These days people don't use money." I tried not to look at Josh, but I could see that he was blushing.

"How strange," said Charlie.

Saturday was a busy day for Charlie. He had all those nice clues with which I had supplied him and it was the weekend that his mother was closing up the Bentley. Although Charlie didn't actually work for his mother, she liked to get a lot of advice, none of which she paid the slightest attention to. On Monday Charlie would get the keys. He kept an eye on the place during the winter, although he was hoping to turn the job over to a guy who sometimes worked for him: Doofus Gillespie.

"Chief Peterson wanted my mother to keep the hotel open for one more week," said Charlie. "He's going to have his retirement parade right downtown on Broadway on Saturday morning and he wanted to cap it off with a brunch at the Bentley."

"A parade?" I said. It would be like Darth Vader having a parade.

"He's served twenty-nine years," said Charlie. "The Chamber of Commerce refers to that time as Saratoga's Renaissance. The Shriners are going to march and they got half a dozen bands and a drum and bugle corps from Albany. There are policemen coming from all over the country. Peterson's going to ride a horse."

"You're kidding."

"A white one. Novack and some other officers will also be on horseback. The mayor will ride on a float. My cousins are all excited about it."

Charlie's three cousins are Saratoga businessmen, good Republicans with hearts of steel and combination locks on their wallets. They saw me as being responsible for leading Charlie astray, which was not too far off the mark given the present state of affairs.

"There's talk that Pataki, the Republican candidate for governor, will make an appearance."

"Sounds like a day made in heaven," I said. "I hope it rains."

It was about ten in the morning and we were having coffee in Janey's kitchen. Josh and Janey had gone out to get supplies for Fleshpot: food, a blanket, a couple of bales of straw, some buckets big enough for him to drink out of. The kids had been using some old dog dishes for the horse, but they didn't quite do the trick. Since all the local horse places had probably been warned by the police to watch out for strange purchases, Janey had driven down to Albany. She had also been muttering about horse diapers and where they might be purchased. After twelve hours her house was developing an equine smell.

The twelve-year-old said, "Isn't it like perfume to your nose?"

The oldest daughter, Emma, brought me a copy of the *Saratogian* when she came back from feeding my cat. You remember how I said that I wanted to appear on the front page of the *Saratogian?* Well, there I was. God knows where they got the picture. Had I had any Halloween pictures taken? It was a night shot, full body, and I was squinting into the camera and my mouth was open. Most likely I was making a wise pronouncement, but it looked like I was saying "Duh." Also I was standing more or less like a gorilla with an underarm itch.

The article said I was wanted for three murders, blah, blah, blah. Chief Peterson said I was armed and should be considered dangerous. No-neck Novack was quoted as saying that I must have "gone clearly around the bend." The scenario was that the Macklin cousins were working for me, but that Harry, or

Bobby, had tried to double-cross me and I had run his Honda off the road with my Yugo. The state police had seen the Yugo leaving the scene of the crime and taken the tag number. Then, not being satisfied with one murder, I had driven to the mill, where I had killed Pennyfeather seemingly for the fun of it, maybe because he had blown up my Yugo. The paper ran a nice picture of him with his Three Stooges haircut prettily combed and no bullet hole between his eyes. I had escaped from the mill in a Dodge Ram four-by-four belonging to Pennyfeather, and I had somehow crammed a half-million-dollar horse into the back of it. Half a dozen people reported having seen the truck with the horse and every single one opined that it was unsafe to transport a horse in such a manner.

The police were also wondering about the whereabouts of Rolf Macklin. That, in fact, was the only good news. No one had seen him with me. On the other hand, fire officials were "combing the debris" of the mill for his corpse, since the possibility remained, said the police, that I had killed him as well. Several people who had known me in Saratoga were interviewed and all three said I was "a strange one" and they weren't too surprised that I had finally "stepped over the line." The general consensus was that I had gone absolutely wacko but that many people had seen it coming.

I have got to say that the *Saratogian* had a lot of fun with these stories. By this time the editor must have had half his staff running around collecting information about Bad Vic Plotz. Clearly, he had visions of Pulitzers waltzing around in his cranium. Like move over, *New York Times*.

Emma read the new stories over my shoulder. When we had finished, she said, "I feel almost proud to know you."

"Too bad my mother's not alive to see this," I said.

"Oh," said Emma, always polite, "has she been dead long?"

"About fifty years," I said.

Charlie had taken Pennyfeather's address book and notebook in order to track down and identify the various people. I imagined him slogging through phone books hour after hour. When Charlie showed up at Janey's that evening around dinnertime, he said that I had worried without cause.

"The phone books are on ROM disks now," he said, rather smugly. "I put in a search for a name or a number and I have the answer in no time."

"I thought you didn't like computers," I said.

"Just because I don't like them doesn't mean I don't use them. They've got all this stuff over at Skidmore."

"So what do you have?"

"I've got a list of about one hundred and fifty people. Now I'll see how many I can eliminate. Some live nowhere nearby, others would have no motive. We should be able to cut it down."

We were having a big spaghetti dinner in Janey's kitchen. Her kids were eating downstairs in the basement with Fleshpot. Josh was eating in the living room, where he could watch a football game on the tube. Charlie, Janey and I were drinking Chianti, one of those squat bottles with string around the bottom so you can't see all the sediment.

"Did the police find the pickup truck?" asked Janey.

Charlie grinned. "Not only that but the desk sergeant received an anonymous phone call suggesting that he check the red paint on the side with the red paint on Bobby's Honda and I guess they did. It looks like they're going to have to revise their theories somewhat."

Josh and I were sleeping up in the attic. None of this was comfortable because we had to stay away from the windows and hide when anyone came to the door. Since Janey's daughters led active social lives, this meant that we were hiding all the time. Fleshpot was more or less settled down in the basement. With three girls to attend to his every whim, the minutes probably did not hang heavy on his hooves.

I spent some time with him on Sunday, giving him an apple, urging him to keep a stiff upper lip. The poor horse probably thought he would never see a grassy pasture again. Charlie found me down there in the early afternoon. He seemed excited.

"I got an old racing program," he said, "and I looked up that ticket. Remember? The fifth race on August 26th, the number four horse to win."

"And did he win?"

"Nope, he came in sixth."

"So why was Pennyfeather hanging on to the ticket?"

"I'm not sure, except the horse belongs to George Slavino."

"The agent who bought Fleshpot?"

"The very same. It seems he owns four or five horses and even trains them. Nothing big-time. At least he didn't have any wins in Saratoga this season."

"Is there anything odd that he should be an agent and also own some horses?"

"Not particularly. It's just odd that Pennyfeather should hang on to the ticket."

"Maybe it's only a coincidence," I suggested.

"In this business," said Charlie in his serious voice, "you get to distrust coincidences."

"Did Pennyfeather have Slavino's phone number by any chance?"

Charlie took off his bifocals and cleaned them on his tie. "As a matter of fact he did," he said.

I gave Fleshpot another apple and he munched it thoughtfully. By now he had about thirty ribbons in his mane and about the same number in his tail. The twelve-year-old was with us and she was grooming the horse's ankles, combing them with a small pink comb. I suppose Fleshpot liked it.

"By the way," said Charlie, "you're going to have to move the horse."

"How come?" I asked.

"It's not private enough here."

"I don't think the kids will say anything," I said.

Charlie motioned over my shoulder and I turned. There were two small windows up near the ceiling. Three girls had their faces pressed to one, four girls had their faces pressed to the other. Not one of the girls was over sixteen. They had rapt, almost devotional expressions. Let me say that it wasn't Charlie, me or the twelve-year-old that they were staring at.

16

I would like to discuss my relationship with keys. Each one's a mystery, right? Which door does it open? And in that way, each key is also a solution. Or at least potentially. Each key is an answer to a big question which may or may not be asked: *Hey, you got the keys?* So I see a key on the sidewalk; I pick it up. Sitting in easy chairs in the houses of friends or hotel lobbies or even sitting in the backseats of cabs, I always dig down into the cushions for the stray key. And when I leave a job, you know how they always say, Don't forget to turn in your keys? I never remember. Consequently, I have a lot of keys. Most are unlabeled and fill half of a bureau drawer. Door keys, padlock keys, luggage keys, jewelry box keys. But I also have a drawer of labeled keys. Like when I was fired from Schultz's Men's Furnishing in New York City back in the mid-sixties, I kept all the keys. Old Schultz died long ago, the business changed hands three or four times, the building was ripped down and a fifty-five-story office tower was built on the exact same spot—I still have the keys.

I left home when I was sixteen, got a job pushing carts in the garment district. My mom was dead, my dad ran a shoe repair shop in Crown Heights. I still have the key to the apartment and to the shoe repair shop. If my dad's coffin had a lock on it, I'd have the key to that as well. I got keys to Charlie's cottage on the lake. I got keys to the Queen of Softness's lunch counter— Rosemary's: Family Eats Can't Be Beat.

What I'm trying to explain to you is that I've got the keys to the Hotel Bentley, which, by six o'clock Sunday evening, was as empty as a pimp's heart.

Charlie was off trying to find some farm or stable to which we could take Fleshpot, but even he was skeptical. "The police are checking all the farms," he told me. "They've even got helicopters."

Stealing a half-million-dollar horse is an even bigger caper than robbing a bank: my name was being bandied about over the TV channels. But sitting in Janey's cellar, watching Fleshpot munch on an apple or the odd carrot or two, it was hard to think of this beast as being equal to four deluxe Rolls-Royces. I can't quite say that Fleshpot had become a pal, a bosom buddy, but already I could look forward to the time when I would miss having him around.

Janey's kids were in bed by nine-thirty, Janey herself was in bed by eleven. From the hall, I watched the crack under her door go dark. I didn't see why Charlie couldn't be chipper in this house. The food was good, the people were *très simpático,* the bourbon was as smoky as elsewhere. Some guys make a romance out of their isolation. They live with their jaws stuck defiantly into the dark. I'm not one of them. Had Janey been a bigger woman, more solid, chunkier, older, bigger breasts, I might have moved in myself.

Josh was dozing in front of the TV. Every now and then I could hear a snort or a clomp from down in the basement. At midnight I decided to get the show on the road.

It was raining. After a perfect August, we were having a dismal September. We put the horse blanket on Fleshpot. Josh heaved a bag of feed over his shoulder. I grabbed a couple of the big rubber buckets and filled both half full with apples. I stuck a brush in my back pocket, then opened the outside cellar door. It creaked and I opened it slowly. We led Fleshpot out into the backyard.

Saratoga was a different town on a rainy Sunday midnight in late September than it had been just a month earlier. On an August midnight the town is full of celebration; on a September midnight the agenda is recuperation. Even the few cars on the streets have guilty looks. Now and then a rat scurries by. The cops, hopefully, are off snoozing in parking lots.

Even so, leading a stolen horse a mile through town is a chancy business. The trouble with a horse is that you can't disguise it as anything else. Add a trunk and call it an elephant? Unlikely. Add a box and call it a Volkswagen? Improbable. I mean, you could possibly disguise the horse by painting stripes on it, but it wouldn't make the horse any less noticeable. If anything, it would stop folks in their tracks, like if I added twenty feet of tubing to the front and twenty feet of tubing to the back and called it a snake.

So we tiptoed. A couple of alleys, a couple of side streets, now and then we stuck to the grass to avoid the telltale "clop, clop," but that of course left hoofprints. I suppose I had to feel grateful for the sedentary life led by most Saratoga Republicans. Like they had gone to bed early in order to build up the energy to grind it to the poor the next day. Shopkeepers need their forty winks. The few lights we passed probably belonged to Democrats, staring sullenly into their whiskey glasses and wondering where the thrill had gone.

We snuck down Railroad Alley, did a rush across Church

Street, cut through some yards at Franklin Square and got over to Railroad Place. Then we worked our way along the alley behind Broadway. Who did we see? A kid on a skateboard in the rain. A guy walking his basset hound, a drunk who bumped into us on Franklin Square and grew indignant.

"Is that the nag I lost a hundred bucks on?" shouted the drunk.

"Nope," I said. "This one's a winner."

"Damn," said the drunk, blowing his nose with his thumb. "I didn't lay eyes on him all season."

We got to the back door of the Bentley and I opened up. It took three keys and I had them all.

"You think there's anything to eat in here?" asked Josh.

"Maybe some crackers."

The electricity was off but I had a flashlight. I don't know if you have ever led a horse up a flight of stairs, but it is a protracted process. First we had to blindfold him again, then Josh would lift his left front hoof and put it on the stair, then the right front hoof and so on. After a while Fleshpot caught on, but he never liked it and his ears went flat back on his handsome head. And he would make those snuffling noises that indicated displeasure. It took us over an hour to get him up to the fifth floor.

You see, although I had keys, I didn't have all the keys. I didn't, for instance, have a passkey. But I did have a key to the honeymoon suite, where the Queen of Softness and I had spent a memorable weekend before the stock market crash. The whole honeymoon suite was done up in red with a gigantic heart-shaped bed and a big heart-shaped tub set into the middle of the floor. Rosemary and I had spent many pleasant moments in that tub playing elevator, and I had to believe that Fleshpot would like it as well.

We reached the suite and I unlocked the door. Josh shut the heavy drapes. I proceeded to draw Fleshpot a bath, then I went in search of some candles. When I returned with candles and a box of Ritz crackers, I found Fleshpot sitting in the bright red heart-shaped tub and there was a lot of water on the floor, which Josh was trying to mop up with towels. But Fleshpot sitting in the tub was a pretty sight. I surrounded him with candles, then fed him apples. He sat on his haunches almost like a dog. The heart was about five feet across. The water was nicely tepid. Now and then Fleshpot would lean forward and sip a little. Then he would whinny. I tossed about a dozen apples in the water and we watched Fleshpot bob for them. Josh nibbled his crackers. I sipped Jack Daniel's from my flask, which I open for emotional occasions. Fleshpot was a young horse, no more than an adolescent, and the world for him was full of fantastic experiences. Tonight a heart-shaped tub was one of them.

"No way!" Charlie kept saying. "No way, my mother would kill me!"

"Charlie," I said, "you're fifty-five, you don't need to worry about your mother anymore."

"Jesus, Victor, you don't know my mother. I'm not worried about a spanking. She'll slap me in jail. Get that horse off the bed!"

It was Monday evening. It had been a long day. You remember that guy who I had been making fun of? The black guy at the yearling sales with the pooper scooper? Like that had been my job for many of Monday's long and dismal hours. Squat and shovel. Let me say that a horse has a thousand qualities but horses cannot be housebroken. They can't even be paper-trained. What are you supposed to do, stick their noses in the mess? And we were on the fifth floor of a hotel. That's a lot of ceilings to ruin. I mean, Fleshpot drank up about half the bathtub, then he proceeded to pee it out. Josh and I were going crazy. This lake of horse urine—it was going to go through the ceiling to the fourth floor, then it was going to go through the ceiling to the third floor, then to the second floor. Right down to the basement. We found mops and pails. We found stacks of newspaper. We found closets full of nice white towels. So that took care of one problem, more or less. But do you think I had any time to investigate any murders? Fat chance.

Josh spent the day, when he wasn't cleaning up after the horse, working with Fleshpot on little tricks. Like he got him to count to three with his hooves. And he got him to shake his head to various trick questions: up and down for yes, sideways for no. These were tricks which he had started teaching Fleshpot out at the mill.

So Josh would ask, "Do you like girls?" And Fleshpot would nod his head to indicate that he did.

And Josh would ask, "Do you smoke cigarettes?" And Fleshpot was shake his head to indicate that he didn't.

But the big thing which Josh did to amuse himself on Monday was to teach Fleshpot to lie down on the heart-shaped bed. And once Fleshpot got the hang of it, I think he rather liked it. I mean, if you want to see Pretty, if you want to see Cute, then you have got to see a cheerful-looking chestnut colt with a mane full of colorful ribbons lying supine on a gigantic heart-shaped bed which is covered with a red satin coverlet. All Fleshpot needed was some black lace underwear.

So this is when Charlie entered the room. I mean, I had telephoned him so he would stop worrying about us. He had no idea where we had gone.

You remember how I told you about the word "nonplus"? Like he did it again. Fleshpot looked up at him demurely from the many heart-shaped pillows. Josh looked proud. I looked chipper. Charlie looked like he had been poleaxed with a two-by-four.

The term "rendered speechless" is another one that I like. I don't believe it has happened to me, but I have been fortunate enough to see it happen to others.

"Hey, Charlie," I said, "we've decided to open a kinky whorehouse."

It was then that Charlie began to make loud noises of protestation. You know the sound a cow makes when you take away her pretty calf in the spring? That's the sound that Charlie made. In fact, Josh was forced to stroke Fleshpot's forehead so he wouldn't get scared.

I had to lead Charlie out of the honeymoon suite. He wasn't himself. It was like dealing with a child. I took him down to the lobby and let him sip at my flask. All the bar liquor was locked away and the Victorian armchairs and couches were covered with white sheets. I positioned Charlie on a couch and sat down next to him.

The Bentley has two big picture windows facing Broadway. Even though the windows were covered with curtains, the light from the street came through them. It was about nine p.m. and there wasn't a lot of traffic. In the off season Saratoga is a big TV town.

"Victor, how did you manage to get in all this trouble?" asked Charlie.

"I guess I was just trying to be helpful," I said. "And one thing led to another."

"The police have been to Janey's. They found evidence of a horse in the basement. And they talked to the neighborhood kids. Janey might be arrested. Peterson's called me twice. He's almost his old self again. I mean, he was shouting. He's positive you want to ruin his retirement parade."

"I wouldn't go near his parade," I said. In fact, I have always hated parades ever since getting lost at the Macy's Thanksgiving Parade when I was a little kid. Because of that experience, a parade to me means thousands of knees poking themselves in your tender face.

"And the hotel, Victor, think of the damage." Charlie was not even looking at me. He was leaning forward with his head in his hands. His porkpie hat was balanced on his bald spot. I patted his back.

"What were my choices, Charlie? I mean, other than sticking a gun to my head and blowing my brains out? I guess it's too bad that I didn't get burned up in the mill."

Although Charlie said, "No, no, not that," he didn't say it as fast as I would have liked. He had to think about it first.

"It just seems," said Charlie, "that there must have been some other choice than putting a horse in my mother's honeymoon suite."

"Those were the keys I had, Charlie. Facts is facts. The best I could do was not to let you know about it, so you wouldn't get blamed."

"Oh, I'll get blamed all right," said Charlie. "Don't you remember what mothers are like?"

"I lost my mother in grade school," I said.

Charlie eyed me as if he thought that this had been a smart decision on my mother's part, as if it had saved her a lot of heartache later on.

"Maybe you're right," said Charlie. "Maybe you didn't have a lot of choices."

"It was the Bentley or jail," I said.

"At least in jail," said Charlie, "you'd be off the street."

"Don't go all Republican on me, Charlie. What are you carrying?" He had some kind of magazine and I thought it was time to change the subject.

"It's the Racing Association's *1994 Media Guide*." He raised it up, then let it drop in his lap. He was still depressed.

"How come? The season's over, unless you're going down to Belmont."

"It's got the pictures and brief biographies of the owners, trainers and jockeys. I got it for George Slavino's picture."

"Let's see," I said.

Charlie began leafing through the Media Guide, which was a glossy production with a spiral binder. Two fire trucks went blaring their noisy way down Broadway, and their revolving lights swept across the darkened lobby of the Bentley, giving Charlie, briefly, a red face.

"Here it is," he said. Charlie had a little flashlight in his hand. He never goes anyplace without a flashlight and an extra handkerchief. The photo was a head-and-shoulders shot. I recognized Slavino from the day that I had tried to get the fake Fleshpot to bite my butt but he wouldn't. Slavino had a long narrow face and a long narrow nose with a bend in the middle. Thin lips, small eyes, big ears. His dark hair was brushed straight back across his scalp and shone as if he still used Vitalis. He had a little smile and deep creases running from his nose to the corners of his mouth. His birth date was February 2, 1952. His birthplace was Queens, New York; his residence Newburgh, New York, and Chestnut Farms in Versailles, Kentucky. He was six feet one and weighed one hundred and fifty pounds.

Under "Family" it said "single." Under "Biggest Stakes Wins," three races were listed: Fatfoot won the Rutgers at Meadowlands in 1989; Harvey's Choice won the Interborough Handicap in 1990; and Bruiser won the Adirondack Stakes in 1991. His only career highlight was that he had won six races at Belmont with a horse named Jolly Peacock. In answer to the question "How Introduced to Racing," he said, "I grew up in New York and hung around Belmont and Aqueduct. After a while I gravitated to the backstretch and started working as a hotwalker for Jimmy Picou." Under "Hobbies," he listed horse breeding and hunting. Under "Likes and Dislikes," he listed winning and losing. Under "Biggest Disappointment," he said, "Losing the Whitney in Saratoga with Bruiser in 1992." Under "Additional Information" it said that Slavino had served in Vietnam in 1971–72 with the 1st Cavalry Division, that he had worked as a professional guide in Montana and Idaho. He had been employed as an assistant trainer for ten years by Woody Kelly, then took out his own trainer's license in 1987 at the age of thirty-five.

I looked at Slavino's face. "He must be a pretty thin guy," I said. I remembered the thin shape I had seen outside the mill on Friday night.

"He's a hunter," said Charlie. "He stays in shape."

"And obviously he knows guns," I said. We looked again at Slavino's photo, his little smile and his long nose, which had been busted at some time in his life.

"I talked to the owner at Henrietta Farms," said Charlie. "His name is Jack Corman. He and Slavino had gone over all the horses in the Fasig-Tipton sales book and had settled on ten possibilities. Altogether Corman was hoping to buy four or five yearlings. They discussed the prices. Slavino had a limit on each horse. Like on one horse, Hip Thirty-four, his limit was a hundred grand. He went up to that point and stopped and the horse sold for one-thirty. On another horse, Hip Ninety-two, Slavino's limit was two-fifty and he got the horse."

"Get to the point," I said.

"Slavino's limit on Fleshpot was four hundred thousand. Even so, he went up to five hundred and thirty thousand. Corman was furious with him. He couldn't see why he did it. Perhaps Slavino was just making certain that he was the one to take over the horse."

"So Slavino's our man?" I asked.

"Not necessarily. I'd like to do a better job of tying him to Pennyfeather. You can help me with that."

"This is more like it," I said. "Just what aspect of my detective genius would be most useful to you?"

"I need the restaurant receipts you got from Pennyfeather's

wallet. Maybe he had one of those meals with Slavino."

You know what it is like to have your greatest skills ignored? "And you can do something for me as well," I said. "We need more horse feed. Otherwise Fleshpot will start eating your mother's drapes."

17

Tuesday night around eleven o'clock I went out for a walk in order to stretch my legs and nose around. It was raining. I had a raincoat and umbrella that I had found in the hotel, although the raincoat was a trifle small and held my underarms in an avid embrace. The wind blew hard from the west, pushing little waves of water across the pavement and shaking the branches of the adolescent maples which had been planted to take the place of the gigantic elms that had once lined Broadway. I walked briskly, the walk of a man with a specific destination in mind: no ambling, no paranoid hurrying. In no time my shoes and the cuffs of my pants were sopping wet. I walked down Broadway toward the Algonquin, my home. The wind tugged at my umbrella but I kept a good grip. No one else was out on the street. A few cars drove by. Only one of the bars was open.

Across from the Algonquin a man was slouched down in the front seat of a black Ford Taurus. He was probably watching to see if the dangerous Vic Plotz entered his building, but he was snoozing instead. I was both flattered that he was keeping an eye out for me and indignant that he was doing a bad job. It's a sign of importance, right, to have your building watched? Why couldn't they hire a crackerjack instead of a doofus? I was tempted to bang on his hood and tell him to straighten up, but, not being much of a runner, I couldn't think what I'd do after that.

I walked around the block and came up toward the Algonquin from behind. The rain was picking up a little. Another guy in a Buick was watching the back entrance. At least he wasn't asleep. He was smoking a pipe and the window was open a crack. His tobacco gave off the smell of apples. I kept going, turned up Lake Avenue past police headquarters, then turned left on Broadway, heading back to the hotel. I needed to make sure that the coppers were actually looking for me so I wouldn't do something stupid like buy a Guinness at the Parting Glass or get breakfast at Bruegger's Bagel Bakery or go chasing around after Pennyfeather's murderer. In store windows and on light poles were posters announcing Harvey L. Peterson's retirement parade on Saturday, which would be followed by an ox roast at Saratoga Spa State Park, rain or shine. All of Harvey's friends were invited to attend. Maybe one, maybe one and a half. By the time I got back to the Bentley, I was sodden.

Josh had begun to take Fleshpot for promenades now, but they stuck to the hotel corridors. Because Fleshpot's hooves might damage the rugs and wooden floors, Josh had tied pillows to them. Fleshpot did not particularly like this, but he adapted. As I said, he was an agreeable horse, but, again, maybe it was his youth. It was all folderol to him. He didn't see the point of pillows on his feet but he was affable. The weird thing about Fleshpot with pillows on his feet was that it made him almost silent. Just shuffle, shuffle—no more.

Fleshpot was also becoming more accustomed to going up and down stairs. He didn't like it and he had to be coaxed, but he could now go upstairs without a blindfold and Josh swore that in two more days he could be taught to go downstairs without a blindfold. Personally, I didn't see how these tricks would be useful in his racing career.

Wednesday morning around nine o'clock Charlie slipped in the back door of the hotel so we could have a little chat. He brought coffee and the three of us had coffee and doughnuts.

"The police have received reports that you and Fleshpot were seen south of Albany," he said. He looked satisfied with this news.

We were downstairs in the bar. Charlie couldn't stand to be up in the honeymoon suite with Fleshpot. He would imagine his mother seeing Fleshpot on the heart-shaped bed—lolling—and get serious chills. Josh had also gotten a bale of hay and had scattered it on the floor and I didn't particularly want Charlie to know this.

"And who was responsible for telling the cops we were south of Albany?" I asked.

Charlie smiled slyly. "At least they won't be looking for you in downtown Saratoga."

There had been no new developments in the case, although, privately, the police were admitting that Bobby's Honda had been knocked off the road by the Dodge Ram four-by-four, which probably had been driven by Pennyfeather. The cops seemed to see this as bad news; it weakened the case against me. I could only be charged with two murders instead of three.

"And I've checked the restaurants," said Charlie. "Pennyfeather and George Slavino had dinner in the Firehouse Restaurant on Friday, August 26th. The same day that Slavino's horse was running in the fifth race. The waitress recognized their pictures." Charlie took a bite of his doughnut, then wiped the powdered sugar from his lips.

"So are you going to drive down to Newburgh and give Slavino the third degree?"

Charlie took another bite of his doughnut, then raised an eyebrow at me. "No, I think we'll go fishing instead."

Josh looked up hopefully. He was getting tired of the hotel and he liked to fish. But I knew that Charlie meant it metaphorically. As he explained what he wanted to do, I grew increasingly unhappy, because if Slavino was the metaphorical fish, then I was to be the metaphorical worm.

"Of course," said Charlie, "you'll have to call the other people as well. We still might be making a mistake about Slavino. You should start right away. Here are the phone numbers." He took a sheet of paper out of the breast pocket of his jacket and gave it to me. "You can be as threatening as you like. They already know you're a crook."

"That's nice," I said. The list contained the names and phone numbers of four people.

"You know there's talk that Clint Eastwood will be taking part in Chief Peterson's parade?" said Charlie. "One lawman saluting another, so to speak."

"Maybe they can get Robocop as well," I suggested. "One metal brain saluting another."

I started making my phone calls from the hotel office right after Charlie left.

The first name on the list was Mrs. Roberta Fielding at Sycamore Farms. I had talked to her before but that had been in the role of a good guy. Now I got to talk to her in the role of a bad guy.

"I just wanted to tell you," I told her, "that the deal fell through with the Chilean. Both Bobby and Pennyfeather are dead, but Pennyfeather said I should call you for new instructions. Josh Flynn is here with me, of course, and we've got the horse in a safe place."

"I beg your pardon?" said Mrs. Fielding. She had a somewhat raspy, elderly voice. I could hear her wheeze as she waited for me to tell her something that made sense.

"We got the horse. Pennyfeather said we should scrag him, maybe cut off his head or shoot him, but I figured we'd give you a chance to buy him back."

"Are you speaking about that chestnut colt?"

"Who else?"

"Then I suggest that you turn him over to the police at your earliest possible convenience."

"And what if it's not convenient?"

We talked like this for a while. She was a feisty old broad and I liked her, but we never reached a point in our relationship where I could suggest that we exchange photos. In any case, it was clear that she had no criminal connection to Fleshpot. When she asked where we were keeping the horse, I said St. Joseph, Missouri, just because Charlie would be pleased to have me shine a little light on Jesse James's hometown.

The agent Henry O'Leary got the next call. He was in his office down in Lexington. A certain amount of my time was spent in conning secretaries and minions, but who cares about that? Why should I explain that five unimportant people were rude to me? What I present here is the *crème de la crème*.

"So I got the horse," I told O'Leary.

I could hear his tweeds shift. "What horse?"

"Fleshpot."

"Fleshpot?"

"Jesus, O'Leary, Hip Fifty-seven, the chestnut colt! You want it or should I kill it?"

I listened to O'Leary breathe, then he said, "Is this Mr. Plutz?"

"Plotz," I said. "Vic Plotz. Pennyfeather told me about your part in the deal before he got shot. And Josh said the same. And I bet Bobby would say the same as well if he weren't dead. The Chilean chickened out and now we're stuck with five hundred and thirty thousand dollars of horseflesh. What should we do?"

"Who's Josh?" asked O'Leary. He spoke like a man whose brain is revolving in a slow wobble.

"You remember Rolf Macklin and his cousin Harry? Their real names are Josh and Bobby Flynn. Don't sweat the small stuff, O'Leary, what should we do with the horse?"

"I suggest you contact the police, Mr. Plotz."

So that was how it went. O'Leary seemed to have no interest in the horse.

"Look, O'Leary," I said, "Pennyfeather said you were to get ten percent, that's twenty-five grand, you just want me to give it to the poor?"

"I suggest you call the police," he repeated.

So that was that.

Next I called Jack Corman at Henrietta Farms in Oxbridge, Kentucky. He must have had a cellular phone and was outside, because I could hear barnyard noises: roosters and a couple of ducks. Now and then a barking dog.

"Hey, Jack," I said, "I got the horse."

"Pardon me?" He had a nice drawl that made me think of Nashville.

"I got the horse, Jack. The chestnut colt. Pennyfeather said I was to call you. Should I talk to Slavino first or are we cutting him out?"

"What in the world are you talking about?" Corman sounded aggravated, as if Ma Bell or MCI had just linked him up with a crazy person.

"Will you stop playing dumb?" I shouted. "Three men have already been killed. I'm holding a half-a-million-dollar piece of property and you want to play cute with me? What if I just called the cops and let them know how you're mixed up in this?"

"Me?"

"Damn straight, Jack. You're just lucky that they don't have capital punishment up here in New York State. Both Josh and Bobby have been talking about you."

"I don't know who you are," said Corman, "but if you have some information which you think the police might want, then I suggest you go to the police and stop bothering me." He cut the connection and I stopped hearing the roosters and ducks.

So then I called George Slavino in Newburgh. His office put me through to his car phone. God knows where he was driving to. I could hear a motor and now and then a big truck.

"George," I said, "we're home clean."

"Who is this?" It was the hushed voice of a man who has been expecting his creditors to call.

"It's Vic Plotz, George. Josh Flynn told me to call you. We got the horse. Should we bring him down to Newburgh?"

"Jesus Christ." There was a silence.

"Hey, George, are you there?"

"What do you mean, Josh told you to call me?"

"Pennyfeather told Josh, Bobby and me that you were part of the deal. Bobby's dead now. He cracked up his car. Josh and I got the horse away from the burning mill the other day. We've been waiting for Pennyfeather but he hasn't contacted us, so I'm calling you to see what you want us to do."

"And who are you?"

"Vic Plotz. I'm the local guy. We got the horse nice and safe, not a mark on him, but we can't hang on to him forever. I mean, he's hot, George."

"When did you come into it?" asked Slavino.

I felt a little hum of pleasure. It sounded as if Slavino had taken the hook.

"Pennyfeather got me after he had dinner with you at the Firehouse at the end of August. He said he wanted someone who knew the local terrain in case there was trouble."

"And why are you calling me?"

There were more truck noises from Slavino's phone. I made groans indicative of exasperation. "Because we're stuck, George. We haven't heard from Pennyfeather. The cops are searching for the horse and we can't just hide out forever."

"Where are you?"

"Up in Saratoga."

"Where in Saratoga?"

"Come on, George, why would I tell you that? We have not yet established a warm and trusting relationship. But let me warn you, if you tell the cops, then me and Josh will tell them what we know. That'll mean serious jail time, my friend. But don't get excited. We just want to get out of here. Josh needs to get back to California. We do a little swap. You get the horse and we get our ten grand. What d'you say?"

"I got to think about it," said Slavino.

"Take all the time you want," I said. "But remember, the cops are looking for us. It'd be too bad for you if we got caught."

"Call me at six." Slavino broke the connection. It seemed that nobody said goodbye anymore.

I called Charlie but there was no answer. It was twelve-thirty and he was probably swimming at the YMCA. He has this fixation where he must spend five or six hours a week dragging his body back and forth through chlorinated water. Like he now smells like a swimming pool. His office smells of chlorine, his cottage smells of chlorine. I bet even the spots where he has caressed Janey Burris's tidy body smell of chlorine. It's perverse.

Having temporarily finished with my phone calls, I went upstairs to check on Josh and Fleshpot. George Slavino had almost put his head in the noose. It might mean that we could soon check out of the hotel.

Josh was now riding bareback up and down the halls. Fleshpot still had the pillows on his feet and it made him walk like a robot.

There were windows at the ends of the hall, but the middle was pretty dim. The head-on silhouette of a horse with pillows on his feet and a rider on his back looked a trifle Martian. I scratched Fleshpot's nose as I told Josh about my various conversations.

"And you never heard the name George Slavino before?" I asked, evading another little duck toward my backside by Fleshpot. Ah, how sweet the flesh must taste.

"Nah," said Josh. "Bobby said I couldn't be trusted with any names. You know, I'm going to miss old Fleshpot. You think there's any chance we could keep him?" He patted Fleshpot's neck and the horse snorted.

"Whopping fat chance."

"Who owns him now?"

"The insurance company, I expect."

"Would they race him?"

"I rather doubt it."

Charlie showed up around three o'clock with a bag of hamburgers and a six-pack of Rolling Rock. I told him about my various telephone conversations, saving the one with Slavino for last. It made him happy.

"When you call him back, get him to come up here," said Charlie. "We'll put a wire on you."

We were sitting in the bar again. It was gloomy and lit only by the lights from the street. "What if Slavino tries to shoot me?" I asked.

"I'll be here and I'll keep him covered. As soon as he incriminates himself on tape, we'll take him into custody. Try to get him to come up as soon as possible."

"Charlie, I still think he'll try to shoot me."

"Relax, it'll be a piece of cake. Did I tell you that Peterson has got Tony Bennett to sing at his ox roast?"

"Fantastic," I said.

"And he's got a Marine drum and bugle corps coming from Washington. I guess Peterson used to be a Marine."

"Makes me proud to live in Saratoga," I said.

"Not only that," said Charlie, "but there will also be a squad of performing Irish setters, because Peterson used to breed setters. They can apparently march in perfect formation without leashes."

"It's great to have a skill," I said.

So at six o'clock I called George Slavino again. No telling where he was, someplace on the highway. I like the idea of driving around the countryside to have a private conversation. You could talk your way straight from Manhattan to L.A.

"A piece of cake," I told him. "You come up here. You give us the ten grand and we'll give you the horse."

"I want to see the horse first to make sure he's okay."

"Sure thing, come up tomorrow."

"I can't do it tomorrow." Slavino paused and I could hear a car honking in the background. "You called Jack Corman," said Slavino. "You shouldn't have done that." There was a coolness to his voice which wasn't due to a lack of interest. It was a mean coolness. I felt its draft on the back of my neck.

"I thought Corman was in on the deal."

"Don't talk to anyone except me," said Slavino.

"So when do I call you next?"

"Tomorrow evening at six."

That would be Thursday. "Why can't you come up tomorrow?" I asked.

Slavino got mad. "You realize that if we don't do this perfectly, we'll go to jail?" I listened to him breathing heavily for a moment, then he broke off.

All this talking on the telephone had got me deeply attached to the instrument, so after I talked to Slavino, I called the Queen of Softness. We chitchatted for a while, then we got down to business.

"Imagine I'm touching you in your secret place," she said.

"Oooo," I said.

"Imagine I'm touching you in your other secret place."

"Ahhh," I said.

"Imagine I'm touching you in your third secret place," she said.

"Just how many secret places do I have?" I asked.

"It depends on how many you want," she said.

The upshot of all this was that around ten o'clock Rosemary picked me up behind the hotel in her big Crown Victoria and we went back to her place to play in her hot tub. We were all nice and wet and warm when the cops pulled up in front of the restaurant. I scooted out the back with nothing more than a towel, then hunkered down in the bushes about a half hour until they went away. It's hard to be an outlaw. I don't know how Jesse James and those guys ever did it. When they finally got shot—John Dillinger, Pretty Boy Floyd—they must have heaved a sigh of relief.

18

F riday morning the banners started going up across Broadway
in Saratoga Springs. I could see them from the front windows
of the Bentley: red, white and blue banners, and red, white and
blue banners on the light poles as well. The banners announced
that Saturday was Harvey L. Peterson Day! Charlie brought me
a *Saratogian* and the entire front page was dedicated to describing
Saturday's events. All downtown stores would be closed between ten and twelve, the time of the parade. The receiving
stand was being erected at the mouth of Congress Park. The
parade was to start at the other end of Broadway, up by the
Skidmore campus. There would be first, second and third prizes
for best float, best band, best baton twirler, best bagpipe player,
best antique car.

After the parade would come the ox roast at the park. Food
was being prepared for several thousand people. The variety of
accolades on the editorial page made Harvey L. Peterson sound
like a mixture of Jesus Christ, Wyatt Earp, Santa Claus and Ro-
nald Reagan. It made me feel proud to have been yelled at by
such a man. His achievement of having been Commissioner of

Public Safety for twenty-nine years was compared to the building of the Statue of Liberty, the Eiffel Tower and the Channel Tunnel. The general consensus was that no one could take his place, for which I heaved a sigh of relief.

There was only one problem. When I had spoken to George Slavino the previous evening, he had said:

"I'll come up on Saturday morning."

"That's not going to be good," I said.

"Why not?"

"We got a parade downtown on Saturday morning. The chief of police is retiring."

Slavino was silent for a moment. "I'm coming up with a horse trailer, but, like I say, I want to see the horse first. What time would be good?"

"Let's say one p.m."

"What time's the parade?"

"Between ten and twelve."

"And you're right downtown?" asked Slavino. "Where specifically?"

"I'll call you Saturday morning and let you know," I had said. "Around ten o'clock."

I had a perverse desire to ask Slavino what it had felt like to shoot Pennyfeather between the eyes, but I withheld myself. Charlie had left the *Media Guide* and every so often I would take a gander at Slavino's picture, look at his thin face and once-busted nose. He was wearing a light-colored shirt with a jacket and striped tie. Under the question "Person Outside of Racing You Most Admire" he had said General George F. Patton.

Charlie was a little unhappy with me. "I wish you hadn't said you were right downtown and that business about the parade."

"Why not mention the parade?"

"Because it gives me a funny feeling."

It was Friday afternoon. Charlie had brought some ice, a big bottle of Jack Daniel's and a bottle of sweet vermouth and we were having Jack Daniel's Manhattans in the bar. He even had a small bottle of maraschino cherries. Josh was upstairs riding Fleshpot. He could now ride him up a flight of stairs but not down. The horse was on his second bushel of apples. I had spent a large chunk of the day, it seemed, cleaning up horse poop. Every time Charlie saw one of these golden nuggets lying on the carpet he would think of his mother and cringe.

"What do you think Slavino's plans are?" I asked, already knowing but not wanting to know.

"I think he wants to shoot you."

"And the horse?"

"He's got no reason to shoot the horse. It can't testify in a court of law. On the other hand, it's too dangerous for him to take the horse since it can be easily identified. I expect he intends just to leave it."

"And Josh?"

"He'll shoot him too. Most likely he will make it look like the two of you shot each other, that you had some kind of quarrel. That way the police won't need to widen the investigation." Charlie sat back in his chair with the tips of his fingers pressed together.

"Tidy," I said.

"But the trouble with letting him know the time of the parade and that you are downtown is that it gives him too much information. The more he knows, the more elaborate he can make his plans. I'd hate to have him kill you, Victor. I mean, you're a pal."

Charlie was having his little joke, but I let it ride. We sipped our drinks as the five-o'clock traffic crawled by the windows of the hotel. From upstairs I heard a whinny. Charlie flinched. I considered the fact of George Slavino wanting to kill me. It gave me a chill in my duodenum.

"What if we just gave all this information to the police?" I suggested.

"Sure," said Charlie, "we could do that. Of course, you and Josh would be arrested. And since one of the charges would be killing Pennyfeather, there wouldn't be bail. The prosecution would probably argue that the two of you killed Pennyfeather in revenge for his killing Bobby. Maybe the prosecution would even accept that Pennyfeather killed Paul Butterworth, maybe not. But there is still the theft of the horse. Josh is clearly guilty of that, and you are tied into it if only as an accomplice after the fact.

"The best you could hope for would be a suspended sentence, and rather large lawyer fees. A grand jury would investigate the accusations against Slavino, but the evidence seems rather circumstantial. After all, why shouldn't he have dinner with Pennyfeather? There could be a hundred innocent reasons why they might see each other. Slavino might beat the charge or he might not, but in any case you'd be looking at quite a long visit in the county jail. How would the Queen of Softness like that?"

More humor, and all of it was supposed to make me feel good about Slavino wanting to kill me. It is like telling the worm, There are dangerous birds who want to eat you; it's safer to try your luck with the fish.

"What time are you going to get here tomorrow?" I asked.

"I still have to pick up the tape recorder down in Albany, but I'll be here by nine-thirty. If I can't make it by then, I'll give you a call. In any case, don't contact Slavino until you've heard from me."

"And you'll let me have a gun?"

"Maybe this time I will," said Charlie.

Let's confess to the unhappy fact that there are two worlds: the world of best intentions and the world of actual occurrences.

In the world of best intentions, when you bet your girlfriend's hefty chest measurements in the exacta, the four and five horses come running in just like they are supposed to. In the world of actual occurrences, they don't. The horses fall down, start to weep, are found at the other end of the track reading a book. Charlie's plan to show up at the hotel on Saturday morning with a tape recorder and a couple of pistols belonged to the world of best intentions. Maybe it would happen, maybe it wouldn't.

As we were sitting in the bar, Josh convinced Fleshpot down the main stairway of the hotel and into the lobby. Because of the pillows on the horse's feet, we didn't hear them until they entered the bar. In fact, Fleshpot snorted about five feet behind Charlie and caused him to spill his drink.

"Can't you keep that horse in the room?" asked Charlie, letting the whine creep into his voice.

"He needs his exercise," said Josh, in his chipper manner. "Going up and down stairs is just like being on a Stairmaster. It keeps the horse in shape."

Fleshpot stood affably looking around the bar, his chestnut coat gleaming in the candlelight. Looking at Charlie, I could tell he was thinking of his mother again. I gave Fleshpot a maraschino cherry, then another. He liked them.

"For God's sake don't do anything to give that horse the runs," said Charlie.

So this is how it went on Saturday morning. First of all, I woke up at six o'clock because the prospect of a day of adventures, including the chance of death, intruded on my sweet dreams. On our first night in the hotel, I had slept in the honeymoon suite along with Fleshpot and Josh. It had not been a success. Even the deepest sleeper would find it difficult sleeping in the proximity of a horse. There is nothing quite like a loud snort at three a.m. to rouse one straight out of bed in the darkness with the burning question: What was that? So I had made myself a sort of bed in a linen closet down the hall which was cramped but serviceable.

After getting dressed, I toddled down to the main lobby to snack on the bagels and cold coffee which Charlie had brought the previous evening. The sun was just coming up and the sky was blue. I imagined the Harvey L. Peterson loyalists heaving a sigh of relief. Their hero had a perfect day for a parade. Good luck for Peterson, bad luck for the cows that were to be roasted out at the state park. Street cleaners had been busy in the night and although Broadway did not actually shimmer with cleanliness, it gleamed a little. Extra trash cans were set out and, by eight o'clock, barriers were erected at the edge of the curb to keep cars from parking and to keep back the millions who would come to see the parade and would most likely mob Harvey L. Peterson and drown him in kisses unless these barriers were in place.

Right at that moment—eight o'clock—Harvey L. Peterson was probably shaving his gray kisser and dabbing his cheeks with aftershave. He was tidying his gray wig and setting it in place with Velcro, or whatever they use. Mrs. Peterson was throwing together a cholesterol-free breakfast for her helpmate. Peterson's classy Irish setters were hanging around feeling proud to know such a man.

Out in the world the baton twirlers were practicing a few last twirls. The marching Marines were probably doing sit-ups or push-ups or whatever marching Marines do first thing in the morning. The hundreds of band members were reviewing their parts, patting their instruments, blowing a couple of the more difficult notes. The marching Irish setters were nosing around Congress Park after squirrels. The mayor was getting ready. The members of the City Council and the Chamber of Commerce were getting ready. Charlie's three successful cousins were getting ready. Out at Lake Saratoga, Charlie was probably standing at the end of his dock sipping his coffee. And George Slavino, what was he doing, that bad man?

Josh got up at nine and came downstairs for cold coffee and bagels. He was barefoot and wore jeans and a ragged white T-shirt. He didn't mind sleeping in the same room with Flesh-pot. He said nothing could bother him when he slept. He went to one of the big picture windows, drew back the curtain a little and looked out. "There're people already waiting for the pa-rade," he said. Then he yawned and scratched under his arm. "I've always liked parades. I'm glad we've got a good view."

By nine-thirty, traffic was blocked off on Broadway. People walked down the middle of the street, half of them were carry-ing multicolored helium balloons with the name "Harvey" printed across them. It occurred to me that all this celebration might be because the City of Saratoga Springs and its citizens were tremendously glad to get rid of Peterson. For twenty-nine years they had suffered under his harsh yoke, etc.

And of course by nine-thirty, I was waiting for Charlie to show up. He didn't. Nine forty-five came and went. Still no Charlie. Minutes crept by. Out on the sidewalk more and more people were gathering for the festivities. Upstairs Josh and Flesh-pot were ambling up and down the halls. At ten o'clock I was supposed to call George Slavino. Over the ornate front desk of the hotel was an ornate antique clock run by a battery. At exactly ten o'clock the telephone rang. Irrationally, I thought it was Slavino. It was Charlie.

"Victor, I had a flat tire coming back from Albany with the tape recorder. I'm in my office. I'll be over right away."

"What are you doing in your office?"

"I needed to get my damn pistol." He described having a flat tire on the Northway and the numbers of people coming into Saratoga for the parade.

"What should I do about Slavino?" I asked.

"Call him right now. I'll be there in five minutes. I'll come through the back." Charlie hung up.

From outside I heard a marching band in the distance playing "Stars and Stripes." Two majorettes hurried along the sidewalk up Broadway holding their red sequined top hats to keep them from falling off. The parade had begun.

When I called Slavino, he picked up on the second ring.

"Do you have the money?" I asked him. I listened for traffic noises but there wasn't any.

"I've got it. Where are you?"

"You know the Hotel Bentley right downtown in Saratoga?" I asked. The marching band was getting closer. The little drums were going ratta-tat-tat-tat and the big drums were going boom-boom-boom.

"You got that horse in a hotel?" Slavino's voice suggested wonder and surprise.

"It's closed for the season. We're here by ourselves."

"You and Josh and the horse?"

"That's right."

"What's all that racket?"

"The parade has started. Why don't you be here at one o'-clock, after the parade is finished. Come through the back."

"Okay," said Slavino. "I should make it by then."

"Are you down in Newburgh?"

"Yeah. I got the horse trailer. I'll drive up right away."

"You'll have to wait until night to take the horse," I said.

"No problem," said Slavino.

After we hung up, I watched the first band march by. In front, four majorettes were holding flags on either side of a banner which read: "Saratoga Springs Salutes Harvey L. Peterson." Then in smaller letters: "Commissioner of Public Safety."

Josh had ridden Fleshpot down the main staircase and now

the horse was off in the dining room walking somewhat awkwardly on his pillowed feet. Josh gave me a couple of apples and I took a bite of one. "I don't think that Fleshpot likes the band music much," said Josh. "His ears keep going back."

We watched a troop of baton twirlers marching six abreast and throwing up their batons in unison, catching them in unison. They wore very short purple uniforms covered with rhinestones and they glittered in the morning sun. The rhinestones made me think of the Queen of Softness, who was most likely someplace in the crowd. The girls also wore little rhinestone-covered caps with black plastic brims. The oldest baton twirler was about twenty, the youngest about six. The last two carried a sign which said: "The Dischell Twirlers, Rhinebeck, New York."

Next came an antique touring car, a bright yellow Stanley with classy black wheels and shining wire spokes. The top was down and the mayor and his wife sat in the backseat and waved to the crowd. There was an ow-ooh-ga horn and it kept going ow-ooh-ga, ow-ooh-ga. People clapped and threw streamers.

When I heard a noise in the back, both Josh and I assumed it was Charlie.

"We're in here," I called.

After the antique Stanley came a large float with a huge papier-mâché rendering of Harvey L. Peterson. It probably stood twenty feet tall and showed Peterson wearing his three-piece blue suit and a cowboy hat. In each of his big hands was a big six-gun. In the corner of his mouth was a big cigar. The cigar and six-guns were smoking.

"Jesus, Charlie, get a load of this," I said, turning around.

It wasn't Charlie. It was George Slavino. He was standing about fifteen feet away. He had a pistol tucked in his belt and he was holding a shotgun. You think he looked friendly? He didn't. In fact, he looked lethal.

19

So this is what happened to Charlie. He got the two pistols from his safe, grabbed the little tape recorder and ran out of his office. Of course, he could hear the parade. The first band went by. The whole space where Phila Street meets Broadway was jammed with people. From where Charlie stood on the sidewalk he could see the batons rising in the air, then falling back again. The mayor passed in his yellow Stanley. People clapped.

Charlie hurried up to Broadway, then began to make his way through the crowd at the curb. Another band was marching past and Charlie thought that once it had gone by, there would be a space which would let him dash across the street. The bass drums went by last: boom, boom, boom. Charlie stepped forward off the curb. The float with the huge papier-mâché statue of Harvey L. Peterson wearing a cowboy hat, smoking a cigar and holding a pair of smoking six-guns, was just approaching. The face on the statue had a sort of self-satisfied grin, as if Harvey L. Peterson were saying: "I done warned you and done warned you, but you did it anyway and so here comes the punishment."

Charlie stepped around the orange barrier that separated him from the street. At that moment someone grabbed his arm.

It was a red-haired police sergeant by the name of Emmett Van Brunt who had joined the department about five years before Charlie had quit. He was wearing a plaid jacket and plaid pants but the two plaids were dissimilar in size, shape and color, and it made Emmett difficult to look at.

"I can't let you cross the street, Charlie," said Emmett.

"I got business over there, Emmett. I've got to cross."

"It'll have to wait, Charlie." Emmett spoke slowly as if each word was the product of serious deliberation.

"It can't wait, Emmett. It's extremely important."

Emmett took out a pair of handcuffs and dangled them before Charlie. "I'd hate to put these on you, Charlie. Look, as soon as the boss goes by, I'll let you cross. But if I let you run across the street in front of his horse, he'd flay me alive. He was saying just yesterday that he was expecting you to fuck up his parade in some nasty way."

"Me?" Charlie told me later that he couldn't imagine why anybody would think he would want to mess with a parade.

"He's warned all of us to keep an eye out. But once he's gone by, then you can scoot across. See, he's coming now."

Emmett was still keeping a tight grip on Charlie's arm. Looking north on Broadway, Charlie saw Peterson up by the Adirondack Trust. He was riding a white horse and he was flanked by two of his lieutenants on black horses: Novack and Ernest Tidings, both ex-military and both weight lifters. In front of them was a Marine drum and bugle corps making a lot of racket with their drums. And in front of the drum and bugle corps were about forty Irish setters high-stepping along to just the occasional command from a couple of trainers: genius dogs who probably read books in their kennels. The dogs were preceded by a troop of Boy Scouts, which was preceded by a troop of majorettes. Passing in front of Charlie were more antique cars with dignitaries waving from rumble seats.

Charlie thought it would take maybe five to ten minutes for Peterson to trot by on his big white horse. Although Charlie was in a hurry, he didn't think he was in a serious hurry. After all, George Slavino was driving up from Newburgh and wasn't supposed to arrive until one o'clock. And Charlie was sort of hurt that Peterson might think that he, Charlie, wanted to ruin his parade. Although Charlie didn't particularly like Peterson, he bore him no malice. After all, let him have his final moment in the sun, his last soupçon of glory.

The dignitary sitting in the rumble seat of the last passing antique automobile was Charlie's cousin Jack, who owned several hardware stores in town. Charlie waved and Jack looked at him suspiciously, which surprised Charlie, who felt that he had always gotten along well with Jack.

The Bentley was right across the street. In front of it stood a crowd of people watching the parade. There was a cool breeze with a hint of winter. The sky was cloudless. October 1st: a nice day, a special day, the sort of day when geese like to travel south.

The Marine drum and bugle corps was making a terrible racket with the bass drums beating steadily and the snare drums weaving patterns on top of them and the bugles blaring away. Charlie was impressed that the Irish setters could stand the noise and he could see their ears twitching unhappily. The majorettes were in front of Charlie now, young girls in pink satin spinning their shiny batons. Charlie glanced up Broadway at Peterson and saw that the police chief had noticed him and was staring at him with suspicion and displeasure. Charlie raised his eyebrows at Peterson to indicate that he meant no harm, even wished him well in fact. Charlie smiled in a friendly manner. After all, in a few more minutes Peterson would ride by and Emmett Van Brunt would let Charlie cross the street.

And Peterson might have believed that smile if other events of a particularly nasty nature hadn't suddenly occurred. First of all, there came a dull explosion from inside the Bentley hotel. One of the big picture windows shattered. People screamed and surged into the street. Charlie slammed his shoe down on Emmett Van Brunt's instep, yanked himself away and tore across the street through the troop of Boy Scouts. At that moment something huge came leaping through the window of the hotel, but I am getting ahead of myself.

I must say that when George Slavino turned up behind Josh and me holding a shotgun and with a pistol stuck in his waistband, I experienced a somber moment. The phrase "the jig is up" passed through my mind. I wish I could confess that my entire life flashed before my eyes, but it didn't.

"Well, well, well," I said, "look who's here."

"Shut up," said Slavino. He was wearing dark brown pants, a dark blue shirt and a dark blue jacket. It occurred to me that he was wearing dark so the blood wouldn't show if any splattered on him. No white shirts for him. Slavino's hair was slicked back and probably stuck in place with bacon grease.

Josh was standing next to me, Slavino was over toward the stairs. "Say, Slavino," I asked, "I been wondering. How'd you get your nose broken?"

"Shut up," he said again.

I have to say that my response to intense fear is to talk like crazy. It's either that or wet my pants. Behind Slavino in the dining room, I could see Fleshpot idly looking in our direction. "A newcomer," he was probably saying to himself.

"So, George," I said, "does this mean that you don't plan to give us the ten grand and take the horse?"

The shotgun was an over-and-under, an ugly thing when stared at from the front. I guessed that Slavino would only shoot one of us with the shotgun, then shoot the other with the pistol, and then make it look like we had shot each other. The trouble was, I didn't see how he could shoot us without attracting a lot of attention from the people outside.

"How could I give you ten grand?" said Slavino. "How could I let you stay alive? A tongue like yours and you'd be talking in no time. It was stupid of you to call Corman." He said this patiently, as if giving a simple math lesson to one of the mentally challenged.

"I'll make a deal with you, Slavino. Give us five grand and you can cut out my tongue, take it home with you to Newburgh."

"You're sick," said Slavino. "It'll be a pleasure to kill you." He took a couple of steps forward.

"I may be sick," I said, "but I'm not a murderer."

We were standing about ten feet from Slavino. Josh was holding himself perfectly still. He didn't look terrified, but neither did he look happy. Fleshpot stuck his head out of the dining-room door. He had a healthy curiosity for a horse and he wanted to check out our new visitor. I still had an apple in my jacket pocket. I took it out and idly tossed it in the air.

"Put that apple down," said Slavino.

"Hey, George, you wouldn't deny your victim a last meal, would you? Is that the pistol you used to kill Pennyfeather?"

"Shut up."

I couldn't think what Slavino was waiting for. Then I heard the drums. The Marine drum and bugle corps was coming down the street. By the time they reached the hotel, they would be making such a racket that a simple shotgun blast would be like a whisper in a shouting match. Fleshpot took a step forward out of the dining room. He had noticed the apple. He had these big white pillows on his feet, although they weren't so white anymore.

"Hey, George, did you like killing Pennyfeather?"

"Shut up."

"George, you can't expect me to stand here and not talk. It's bad enough to be shot, I don't want to be bored as well." All this time I was tossing the apple. Fleshpot took another step into the hall, then another. I didn't look at the horse directly, I didn't want Slavino to know he was there. Josh was also watching the horse out of the corner of his eye. If the chance arose for someone to move quickly, then Josh would have to be the guy to do it, because my days of quickness were over, or so I thought.

"And did you kill Butterworth as well?"

"I don't know what you're talking about."

"And the mill, did you burn the mill?"

Slavino raised the shotgun. "Didn't I tell you to shut up?"

But he didn't shoot. The drum and bugle corps wasn't close enough yet. I kept tossing the apple. Fleshpot took another step forward.

"George, we can't stand here doing nothing, the tension will be the end of me. Why don't we play echolalia."

"What's that?" asked Slavino.

I kept tossing the apple. "That?" I said.

"Yeah, what's echolalia?" Fleshpot was four feet behind Slavino. Did he have an eager look in his eye? I hoped so.

"Echolalia?" I asked.

"Yeah," said Slavino, "what is it?"

Fleshpot took another step.

"It?" I asked.

The drum and bugle corps was getting louder. "Goddam you, Plotz," said Slavino.

At that moment Fleshpot leaned forward and bit Mr. George Slavino on the backside. Chomp!

Well, the next few seconds saw a lot of activity. First of all, Slavino elevated. He rose in the air as if yanked by cables from above. And as he elevated, he turned to the left, and as he turned to the left, he fired the shotgun, accidentally, I expect, because his face was going through a contortion suggestive of pain. The shotgun spray missed us by quite a few feet but it hit the drapery covering the picture window head on, with the result that the drapery was torn away and the window shattered outward. People screamed.

At that same moment, Josh dove forward toward Slavino. He dove forward and Fleshpot dove forward but they were going in opposite directions. Fleshpot had not liked the shotgun exploding a foot or two from his delicate ears and it put him in a tizzy, meaning he wanted to get out of there, and suddenly he saw the open picture window and the street lying beyond. As the horse leapt forward, he gave Slavino a knock, sending him staggering toward Josh. That was the last I saw of either Josh or Slavino, because Fleshpot was charging the window with those big pillows on his feet and I jumped over to intercept him, meaning to grab his bridle. Outside, people were still screaming and carrying on.

I don't know if you have ever attempted to intercept a charging horse, but the animal has got a lot of momentum. I grabbed the bridle with my right hand and was immediately yanked off my feet. There were some soft armchairs in the lobby and Fleshpot ran right between them. Me, I dashed up one of them, still hanging on to Fleshpot, who was dragging me forward. My feet hit the cushion, then the top of the chair, just like a ladder, and suddenly I was on Fleshpot's back with my arms wrapped around his neck and my feet tucked under his belly. That was how we went through the window. And that was when I saw Charlie, barreling across the street with a pistol in each hand and all these terrified Boy Scouts diving in every direction. A paranoid, victimized lot they must have been.

I swear, my only intention was not to fall on my head. I had absolutely no wish to interfere with Peterson's parade. But suddenly Fleshpot was in the middle of about a hundred Irish setters who started barking and leaping and rushing around. I don't know if you have ever been intimate with an Irish setter but they can be very hysterical. In fact, an Irish setter is just a furry chunk of hysteria waiting to happen. Fleshpot didn't like this one bit. He was hopping up and down with those damn pillows on his feet, kicking out, but not doing the dogs any harm, whinnying wildly, sending the dogs flying through the air: pillow-booted, feather-whacked into the crowd of people standing at the curb, although they were standing still no longer. Let me say that the variety of sounds formed a cacophony which the composer Charles Ives would have felt proud to have created. As for me, I hung on tight as the horse continued to bounce.

Fleshpot didn't bounce for long, however. It must have become clear to him that the only way to avoid those dogs was to run, so he ran. If he had run toward the sidewalk or if he had run in the direction that the parade was going, it might not have been a big problem. But he decided to run against the traffic. Maybe he saw those three horses being ridden by Peterson, No-neck Novack and Tidings. Maybe he acted impulsively. He ran, and I, in a manner of speaking, ran with him.

Now a parade is a tricky business, because it has no brain. So when the front part of the parade stops, the back part might still be marching. This creates a certain density in the middle, and it was toward this crowded middle that Fleshpot made his way, feet flying, or, as it were, pillows flying. I guess there must be something keenly terrifying about a horse with four big pillows strapped to his feet and a gray old fart like myself clinging to his back somewhat the way the leeches clung to the back of Humphrey Bogart in *The African Queen*.

First of all, the Marine drum and bugle corps scattered. They didn't quite put down their instruments, but they did leave them lying helter-skelter in the street. Fleshpot managed to give a bass drum a kick and I saw it flying into the crowd. Bugles clattered around his feet like fallen leaves. I had a sense of what Moses had felt when the Red Sea split in front of him. But on the other side of this sea of Marines with their blue jackets and flying red caps was not the Promised Land, only Harvey L. Peterson sitting frozen on a big white horse.

The word "awestruck" is a good word to use to describe Peterson's condition. His eyes did not leave his head, but it was clear they wanted to. His cowboy hat fell off. His white horse was doing a kind of high-stepping nervous dance, because he knew hysteria when he saw it, and a lot of it was coming in his direction. Fleshpot did not pause. In fact, he showed that speed which had led a lot of people to think he was worth half a million dollars. It was like the Assyrians coming down like the wolf on the fold.

Even though my face was buried in Fleshpot's mane, I could see Peterson staring at me as we rushed toward him. His gray wig had slipped to one side of his head and had a jaunty aspect, somewhat like a gray beret. Over the frantic shouting and screaming, over the barking of the dogs, over the noise of the approaching bands who had not yet figured out that something had gang awry, I heard Peterson shout, "You, you!"

And then we were among them. Fleshpot was bucking and jumping. The horses with No-neck Novack and Tidings immediately dumped their precious charges onto the concrete. Peterson kept his saddle but he had a hard time doing it, because his white horse was doing a step that combined the tap dance and samba. His wig imitated the pigeons and sailed away. I wish I could say that I knew what happened to Peterson next, but after twirling around a few more times, Fleshpot continued his rapid progression through the parade. There was a series of facial expressions which I came to recognize: curious wonder, sudden recognition, stark terror, and the wish to escape. It was a four-step process which I saw on several hundred faces as we made our swift journey up Broadway.

Bands scattered. The Lions Club contingent broke ranks and dove, individually, for the curb. I saw Charlie's cousin Robert land on his belly. The Elks Club contingent changed from a disciplined mass into thrown confetti. The Shriners' purple Turkish fezes with their tidy tassels went flying and became so much clutter around Fleshpot's pillowed feet. The Shriners dropped their bagpipes. Majorettes dropped their batons. Antique cars drove into the crowd making ow-ooh-gah noises. A horse-drawn float with a gigantic sign reading "Harvey L. Peterson, Twenty-nine wonderful years" veered toward the curb as the horses went out of control. The float was tipping over as Fleshpot and I passed by.

There were other floats commemorating significant events in Peterson's career: the arrest of a bank robber, the arrest of a car thief, the discovery of a lost boy in the hills outside of town. These veered sharply to the left or right. Let me say that flimsily constructed floats are not designed to take sudden movements. The scantily clad women fell off; the papier-mâché figures collapsed.

"Victor, Victor!" I heard someone shout.

Glancing between Fleshpot's ears, I saw the Queen of Softness standing on the curb. She was wearing an orange satin dress and she was waving to me. Her face showed such concern, such love, that I proudly waved my hand to her and tried to blow her a kiss. That was when I fell off.

20

The spanking new van that I purchased had tinted windows—blue to match my pal Charlie's eyes—and it would take a guy with a searchlight to see who was sitting in the driver's seat. There were no windows in the back, just four easy chairs and a table. Like the van was a kind of secret clubhouse on wheels. On Wednesday morning, October 5th, it was parked outside the Spa City Diner with Charlie and me sitting in the back, waiting for Rosemary and Janey Burris, who were inside the restaurant ordering four breakfasts to go. I had been advised that it was not safe for me to go into the restaurant. Harvey L. Peterson had friends everywhere and I might get pummeled. This struck me as unfair. Hadn't I, I wanted to ask, helped arrest a desperate murderer and rescued a very expensive wonder horse? Didn't I have bruises on every inch of my body and a broken collarbone? It made no difference. Harvey L. Peterson's friends were cut from the same cloth as their hero, meaning they were stupid.

The Saratoga and Albany papers had gotten a lot of good photographs of Saturday morning's debacle and a kid with a videocamera had made a bundle selling dramatic footage to the

TV stations. In my opinion, I should have gotten a percentage, but my suggestion wasn't taken seriously. Considering that his video would have been worthless without me, I felt I had a point. After all, hadn't I upstaged Peterson and become the parade's star?

As I had been galloping Fleshpot down the street, Charlie had dashed into the hotel, jumping through the very window that Fleshpot had jumped out of. He got there in time to see Josh and Slavino wrestling on the floor and Josh getting the worst of it. Charlie proceeded to show Slavino his pistol and Slavino realized that his life of crime was over. Then Charlie handcuffed him. Charlie loves cop paraphernalia. I'm surprised he didn't Mace him as well.

A number of people had been cut by flying glass and the ambulances began to arrive. Because the buckshot hit the drapery before it hit the window, the carnage was less than it might have been. Still, there was blood on the sacred sidewalks of Saratoga Springs. Human gore. I was loaded into an ambulance too, which was just as well because otherwise I might have been mistreated by the unruly crowd. The Queen of Softness had gotten into the ambulance with me.

"I hadn't realized that you hated Chief Peterson quite so much," she said, soothing my brow with a hankie dipped in Chanel No. 5, a present I had given her before the stock market crash.

I tried to explain that my actions were not intended to reflect any personal emotions. It was mere chance that I had galloped through Peterson's retirement parade. Bad karma, an unlucky coincidence. Had I been offered a choice, I would have preferred not to do it. After Fleshpot had dumped me rather unceremoniously onto the roadway, he had galloped forward, disrupted several more bands, prompted more majorettes to flee, caused a float—which displayed a tall and half-clad woman posing as blind justice with her scales—to overturn and forced a

Model T Ford to run into a bush. Then, having made his emotional statement, Fleshpot had stopped and begun to munch grass. After about ten minutes he was led away, quite docile.

There was much loose talk as to who bore responsibility for the damage, but that became focused on someone other than yours truly once it became known that George Slavino had fired the shotgun which had terrified the horse. It was never explained that Slavino fired the shotgun because Fleshpot had solidly nipped his backside. That should remain our secret. Much was made of the fact that Harvey L. Peterson had managed to retain his seat in the saddle, despite his panicky horse, and had not been dumped on the pavement like his aides, No-neck Novack and Lieutenant Tidings. For this flimsy shred of distinction the Commissioner of Public Safety was grateful. "At least I wasn't thrown from my horse like those other guys," he said about two hundred times.

Charlie was celebrated for catching a dangerous criminal. Josh was celebrated for jumping on an armed man. And I, well, I wasn't celebrated at all, which was why I had to buy this van. My intention, of course, had been to stop the horse from dashing out of the hotel and rushing into the crowd. And I think it was quite brave of me to fling myself in the path of a stampeding animal with no thought of the consequences, but never mind.

There was a knock on the side of the van and I slid the door open a crack. It was Janey and the Queen of Softness with our breakfast. I let them in and they began to distribute the food on the table: blueberry pancakes with syrup, orange juice, coffee, sausage and bacon.

"No napkins?" I asked.

Rosemary withdrew them from her cleavage. Janey had the milk and sugar for Rosemary's coffee. Once we were settled and had begun to eat, Rosemary asked, "Did that dear boy get out of jail?"

"The prosecutor decided to drop the charges," said Charlie.

"He's gone with the horse down to Oxbridge, Kentucky."

Josh had been jailed for his part in the theft, but then the prosecutor had been convinced that Josh knew practically nothing about any criminal activity and after all he had risked his life to capture Slavino. It was felt that no jury would convict him and the prosecutor had spoken of the unnecessary expense of bringing him to trial since a conviction was impossible.

Jack Corman of Henrietta Farms reached a deal with the insurance company and had taken possession of Fleshpot. Josh had been part of the deal and now had a new employer. Because of the chance that Fleshpot had been damaged or corrupted or spoiled, Henrietta Farms had only given the insurance company $400,000 for the horse, although Fleshpot had seemed pretty quick to me. The insurance company was glad to get the money and Corman was glad to get such a bargain. After all, it was the price which he had originally told Slavino not to exceed.

"I still think you should have given Josh half of the money those insurance people gave you," Rosemary told me, then she pouted.

"He was my employee," I said, trying to sound like a bored yet determined explainer of the obvious. "Consequently, I gave him ten percent of my ten percent."

Outwardly I remained cool; inwardly I was singing Bach chorales. The insurance company had had a ten percent reward for the return of the horse: that's ten percent of five hundred and thirty thousand dollars. I was due to get the money sometime this week. It had paid for the van, and I had also given five thousand dollars to Josh, not telling him, of course, about the fifty-three thousand, since I didn't want to embitter the poor boy. Better to have him feel grateful for the pittance he had received than grouchy about the prize he had missed. In any case, he had a lifetime of honest labor in front of him, whereas I had to think of my twilight years. Three thousand down for the van left me forty-five thousand smackers: a sufficient chunk of change to make me once again an active player in the stock market. Wall Street, watch out.

"I didn't get anything," said Charlie.

"Don't be silly," I told him. "You're getting a free breakfast."

George Slavino was in jail. The pistol he had been carrying turned out to be the same gun that killed Pennyfeather. And it was determined that Pennyfeather had killed Paul Butterworth by slugging him with a two-by-four after Butterworth had seen the horses exchanged. Traces of Butterworth's blood had been found in one of the stalls in Barn Three West. The police couldn't connect Slavino to the murder except as an accessory after the fact because Slavino had been at the auction until midnight and hadn't left the Pavilion.

Among Slavino's papers was found the name of the wealthy Chilean who had intended to buy Fleshpot. He had been contacted by the FBI and he offered to provide a large body of damning evidence, although he said he had not known the horse was stolen. He acted shocked about this. Isn't it wonderful how we continue protesting our innocence right to the very end? "Not me," we tell Saint Peter, "it must have been somebody else."

There was talk in town about giving Peterson another parade, but he said that he didn't want one. Even if it could be guaranteed that I would be in jail, he still didn't want to march down Broadway again on a white stallion. Poor man, in a way his spirit had been broken. When I happened to see him in police headquarters, he was mumbling to himself and had cracker crumbs on the lapels of his blue suit. He didn't see me, but I believe that if he *had* seen me, he would have begun to whimper.

"The main news," said Charlie, finishing his coffee, "hasn't anything to do with George Slavino or Fleshpot or Peterson or anything. The main news is that I'm going to be moving into

Janey's house." He said this with a big smile, but there was an edge to his voice.

"You're getting married?" asked Rosemary, delighted.

"Not yet." Charlie looked nervous about that prospect. "We just want to live together and see how it goes."

"What about those three noisy girls?" I asked.

"I love them all," said Charlie.

"Yes, but what about their noise?"

Charlie raised his shoulders and let them drop. "Stereo headphones, I guess."

Janey was grinning. "He'll still have his cottage on the lake and he can go back there to recuperate anytime he likes."

"Like six days out of seven," I said.

"Not at all," said Charlie. "I'm really looking forward to this." Then he gave me a little twist of the knife. "What about you, Victor, when can we see you moving in with Rosemary?"

Various phrases occurred to me. When hell freezes over, or When the dead are reborn again and walk the streets of Saratoga.

"Moshe's a town cat," I said. "The country would drive him crazy."

"Actually, I prefer our relationship as it is," said Rosemary. "Vic being in town means that I can still go out with other men, if I choose to." She heaved her bosom, then looked to the right and left.

"What?" I said. "What?"

"There's a state trooper who has taken to stopping by two or three times a day for his coffee," said Rosemary.

"They carry diseases," I said. "Virtue, honor, fidelity. You can catch a bug."

"And have you finished cleaning the hotel?" asked Janey, tactfully changing the subject.

"Just about," I said. "I need to touch up some wallpaper in the honeymoon suite." Cleaning the hotel had been the extent of my punishment. If I made everything neat and shiny again, Charlie promised not to tell his mother, who, unfortunately, would have pressed charges. Actually I had hired a couple of guys, which would take a thousand bucks out of my forty-five thousand. A trifle. I felt somewhat smug. I had solved the case, more or less, and had come away with a bundle of cash. Good times lay ahead.

At that moment there was another knocking on the side of the van. I slid open the door, assuming it was a waitress with more coffee.

It was a small bald man in his fifties in a brown suit. At first I couldn't place him, then I realized it was Arnold Steinfeld, the lawyer. I started to slide the door shut but he put his foot in the way.

"I see that you have come into some money, Mr. Plotz." He gave a smile which was basically just exercising his cheek muscles in that it contained neither humor nor warmth.

"Are you kidding?" I said indignantly. "I don't have a dime to my name."

Another smile. "That is not what you have been telling your cronies at the Parting Glass. I believe that fifty-three thousand dollars was the sum you were bragging about."

Now here is one of the world's great unfairnesses. If you never speak of your great deeds, then people cannot pat you on the back and tell you how wonderful you are. But if you *do* speak of your great deeds, then someone is going to try and snatch your greatness from you.

"Have you forgotten your creditors, Mr. Plotz?" He smiled a third time. I wanted to tell him not to bother with the smiles because they would only wrinkle his already wrinkled puss, but my mind was in the grip of other subjects.

"What creditors?" I asked.

Steinfeld held out a piece of paper and, foolishly, I took it.

"The ones whose names are mentioned in this subpoena," he said. Then he made a little bow and slowly shut the door.

There was a chuckling behind me. My dear friends were finding the situation humorous.

"Easy come," said Charlie, "easy go."

I began to make several comments about the spurious originality of his remark and I turned to face him. He had a cheerful smile, but it was also kindly and even sympathetic. His gray hair was sticking up, his eyes were crinkled at the edges, his bifocals had their customary smears. For this celebratory breakfast occasion he was wearing a striped tie that must have spent most of its long life serving as a dog's leash: a big dog that pulled a lot. I thought again how much I liked him. Then, in the interests of friendship, I kept my mouth shut.